Juggling Fire

JOANNE BELL

ORCA BOOK PUBLISHERS

Library and Archives Canada Cataloguing in Publication

Bell, Joanne, 1956-
Juggling fire / written by Joanne Bell.

ISBN 978-1-55469-094-7

I. Title.

PS8603.E52J85 2009   jC813'.6   C2009-903348-8

First published in the United States, 2009

Library of Congress Control Number: 2009929362

Summary: Sixteen-year-old Rachel embarks on a solo quest to find her father,
who disappeared years ago in the Yukon wilderness.

Orca Book Publishers gratefully acknowledges the support for its publishing programs
provided by the following agencies: the Government of Canada through the Book Publishing
Industry Development Program and the Canada Council for the Arts, and the Province of
British Columbia through the BC Arts Council and the Book Publishing Tax Credit.

"Do Not Go Gentle Into That Good Night" by Dylan Thomas, from *The Poems of
Dylan Thomas*, copyright © 1952 by Dylan Thomas. Reprinted by permission of
New Directions Publishing Corp.

Design by Teresa Bubela
Cover artwork by Getty Images
Author photo by Mikin Bilina

ORCA BOOK PUBLISHERS
PO Box 5626, STN. B
VICTORIA, BC CANADA
V8R 6S4

ORCA BOOK PUBLISHERS
PO Box 468
CUSTER, WA USA
98240-0468

www.orcabook.com
Printed and bound in Canada.
Printed on 100% PCW recycled paper.

12 11 10 09 • 4 3 2 1

For Mary with thanks

DO NOT GO GENTLE INTO THAT GOOD NIGHT

(stanzas four through six)

Wild men who caught and sang the sun in flight,
And learn, too late, they grieved it on its way,
Do not go gentle into that good night.

Grave men, near death, who see with blinding sight,
Blind eyes could blaze like meteors and be gay,
Rage, rage against the dying of the light.

And you, my father, there on the sad height,
Curse, bless me now with your fierce tears, I pray.
Do not go gentle into that good night,
Rage, rage against the dying of the light.

—Dylan Thomas

Contents

PART 1

Into That Good Night

Juggling Fire

Mom doesn't cry when I heave the packs from the pickup; she only blinks hard, squeezes my shoulders and whirls around, like she has to get away from me fast. If I didn't know her so well, I'd say she was furious. Her face is too tight to figure out.

My older sister Becky, however, hugs me until my backbone cracks.

I gasp.

"THAT doesn't hurt, Rachel," she scoffs.

Before I can squeeze out enough breath to yell, she sticks a bag of caramels and a roll of duct tape in my pack's side pocket. "Got any haywire for Mom's muffler?"

I shake my head, mentally rolling my eyes. Really! As if I won't need it more than they will. If I had haywire, I'd hang on to it.

"Come back alive," she suggests cheerfully. She removes the caramels, bites open the bag, extracts a palmful for the ride back to town and sticks the remaining candies back in my shirt pocket. "Might be a long, slow drive," she remarks, rolling her eyes toward Mom. "We'll need a bite of trail food ourselves."

Mom's head is resting on the steering wheel.

"Mom?"

She lifts her head and nods with a small smile. "I love you," she mouths through the window.

Then she starts the engine.

"Me too," says Becky. "Got to go."

She bangs the passenger door shut, rattling the whole truck.

Mom grinds the gears and leans on the horn. Brooks, who is a nervous but sweet dog, crouches, shaking, behind my legs. Lots of things make him shake. Our red pickup bumps and backfires down the gravel mountain road away from me, belching black smoke. The smell of burning brakes drifts over the Yukon tundra, and it sounds like the muffler's falling off. Mom never did pay much attention to anything mechanical. She's an artist. The details of everyday life don't interest her much.

I stare until the truck is out of sight, swallowed by scarlet dwarf-birch leaves and yellow willows. Neither Mom nor Becky leans out to wave at me. To be fair, Mom doesn't want to start begging me to stay. This trip of mine is her worst nightmare come true.

Brooks, still cowering behind me, and I are finally on our own.

I've wanted to do this since I was a little kid. I'm sixteen now, so I've waited for almost ten years.

"Come on, boy," I mutter, balancing the two sides of his pack bags in my hands to be sure they're even. "Time to stand up."

Eyeing his load, Brooks slinks to the ground and sweeps his tail hopefully at me. "Not a chance, buddy." Brooks makes a sound in his throat like a siren warming up, staring at the ribbon of gravel where scattered puffs of exhaust are still floating away. He hates to see anyone in our family leave. Brooks's idea of a good time is to sprawl by the woodstove with the three of us in sight.

"Up." I haul him to his feet and buckle the straps under his belly. Breathing in a faint smell of sun and warm dog fur, I snap the final strap around his chest. Brooks at once sinks back down and tucks his head out of sight under his paws.

My stomach clenches. Why am I doing this? I'm not sure I want to anymore.

My pack's too heavy to lift. I crouch down to slip the straps under my arms and, using Brooks's skull as a lever, push myself to my feet. Sucking in my stomach, I cinch the belt tight around my hips and buckle up.

No way. I'll never make it a mile with this load. Panic gusts through me.

I stick my hands under the shoulder straps and lean forward until my breathing slows and deepens. "One step at a time," I tell Brooks, coaxing him to his feet.

He promptly collapses.

Breathe slowly, I tell myself. I gaze around me. Sunlight lights up a boulder on the slope to my left. For a moment I'm sure it's a grizzly.

Fear flames from the pit of my stomach up my chest and into my throat. My eyes skitter over the tundra. I feel like a flushed calf streaking to safety. I can be prey here, just like a yearling caribou I saw once, picked over by wolves. Only my jawbone and maybe a hunk of boot will be left.

"Enough," I say out loud. "Lightning kills more people than grizzly bears do. So does panic. Let's go, boy."

Brooks is bunched in such a tight ball that I can't find his head. I manage to haul him up again by heaving on his pack straps without taking off my own load.

Leading him away from the road, I start down the trail before he has a chance to dig in his paws. Brooks tramps reluctantly at my side, occasionally bumping against my legs, staring pitifully up into my face and whining to make sure I know he's not into this.

Because we're on top of a mountain pass, the tundra is spread out for many miles around us. I can see down the sweep of mountains to where we'll be walking tomorrow. No real trees grow here; the largest shrubs are waist-high clumps of willow and dwarf birch. Out of habit, I trail my fingers along a birch stem. Sandpaper-rough birch twigs scratch my bare legs like thorns.

I could just go home.

A wedge of cranes creaks through the sky; they sound like a chorus of screen doors slamming shut.

It wouldn't help. I'd still need to do this.

Brooks is half bloodhound and half malamute/Newfoundland cross. His father is Chili, Becky's wheel dog, the last and usually the strongest dog in the team. Chili's mother is Becky's old lead dog, Ginger, and Chili's father was Dad's lead dog, Bear, who died one spring day not far from here.

Brooks's mother is a purebred bloodhound who got loose and came sniffing into Becky's dog yard, hunting for a mate. Becky and I had just been returning from a walk with Chili. We looked at each other and laughed, and without a word, she unsnapped Chili's leash. The bloodhound's owner was relieved to have a good home for a pup. It's hard to imagine my life without Brooks.

Brooks has a sled dog's powerful chest and legs, a long thin nose shaped like an icicle, and glacier blue eyes, but weirdly enough, he also has the sagging eyelids, pouches of hanging skin and droopy ears of a hound. Brooks, even when cheerfully chasing rabbits, looks so sad that I hug him every chance I get. He can howl like a husky and bay like a hunting dog. When I hug Brooks, he goes limp, squeezes his eyes closed and sighs with pleasure. Brooks is about as mean and tough as a spring snowball melting into mush.

My hands are moving along Brooks's head. He nudges me with his nose, hoping for a change of heart. When I keep walking, he dredges up a series of deep mournful bays.

I ignore him. The pack bulges from both his sides, hanging from the ridge of his backbone. He waddles and bumps, but at least he's staying close.

She has to be nuts. What kind of mother would let me go?

"I'll give you a month," Mom said.

"Give me?"

She gouged a minute speck of wood from the caribou she was shaping. "If I flew in a month after you got there, you might be ready for company." She held the carving in front of her face with both hands and gently blew at the shavings. I watched them float a moment in a shaft of sunlight before they slowly sank to the floor.

That's what she's usually like. Mom's always had a pretty clear sense of when I need to do something, which battles are hers to fight and which are mine. But she also respects me. That's obvious. And because she does, I agreed.

I let her show me what to pack. She suggested lots of high-calorie foods: butter, chocolate, cheese and nuts. I agreed to it all.

I hardly eat anything anyway. I don't need to eat much. It's probably bragging to say this, but I'm thin and supple—kind of like a green willow, Becky says. I'm not anorexic or anything. I just don't get hungry too often, which is weird because I'm extremely tall and, unfortunately, still growing. When I stand beside Mom or Becky, I find myself hunching over so I don't feel so awkward. All my life I was little, and then last year I grew five inches in nine months. I don't like it much; I feel like I grew out of myself.

Sometimes I forget to eat all day. Then at night, I can't. It's weird actually. I look at food and know it will taste good, but somehow I can't put it in my mouth. Or I just put in a taste and then my throat clenches shut.

Mom said when I was little I had chubby cheeks and I wanted to be a gymnast. She said I was smart and kind of—jolly. These days I have no idea what I'm going to be. I mean, I juggle and I memorize fairy tales. How can I make a life from that? I really do memorize them—page by page. And when I've got them memorized, then I change them.

As Brooks and I bump along, I start to recite a story from an old Irish fairy-tale book Mom read to us when I was small. The original was called "The Princess in the Glass Tower." My version, which is evolving every time I tell it, is called "When the Princess Bolted from the Palace."

In the original story a beautiful princess is on display in a glass castle on top of a glass hill. Her father, the king, has decreed that to win her hand and the kingdom, a prince must ride to the top of the hill. This has proven rather difficult, as the king has also decreed that unsuccessful suitors will be either put to death or locked in chains in the dungeon. Unless, of course, they can out-gallop his pursuing knights.

I haven't looked at the original story for many years. It's gone through so many versions, first Mom's and then mine. How do I know what the original story said? Whenever I read a fairy tale that I love—modern or traditional—it reminds me of that first collection of Irish tales. It had black-and-white illustrations and big letters and old-fashioned language. Not just the choice of words was archaic, but the way the sentences were put together. The other thing I remember is that the characters were fearless and stubborn in the face of danger. If they were scared, they stood straighter and whistled in the wind.

The illustrations were just sketches really. Sometimes Becky and I took crayons and colored them in. The sky here is peacock blue streaked with snowy white. The ground cover is rusty nail brown, apple scarlet, banana yellow and wine purple. It looks like Becky and I were let loose with that pack of wax crayons one last time. I laugh out loud and feel my muscles unclench as I trudge on.

✳

By the time I get to the part where the various princes are lined up to die with their steeds on the glass hill beneath the princess's window, I'm hiking down the pass. I force myself not to check for anything moving. It would be easy to get paranoid out here.

The land is orderly beneath us. Lines of yellow willows outline creeks, dwarf birch defines the tundra, and scarlet berries outline the higher dry knolls. Wizened fireweed stems stand close by. The ground is littered with four-sided stalks of heath shaped like screwdriver handles stuck in the moss.

The princess is getting enormously frustrated waiting on top of her glass hill. It's no kind of life. Something has to happen and soon. It's time to change the ending.

✳

The princess leaned out the window of her glass prison and watched the princes below. At least they were free, she thought.

The princes wheeled their steeds into a circle. In the circle's center was the youngest and fairest, bare-headed and lean, with the look of sunshine and happiness and the open forest in his smile. He looked up into her face as if asking a question.

From her glass pinnacle, the princess nodded.

The youngest prince raised his sword in a salute and dug in his heels. The corner of his mouth tugged up along with one eyebrow, and he lifted the reins to charge the slope.

Before his steed even moved, the princess climbed out the window and slid down to meet him. Holding her skirts, she raced across the palace grounds to the circle of princes, grabbed the reins from the youngest prince and vaulted into the saddle in front of him.

It was that simple. She'd only had to choose.

The prince with the look of sunshine and happiness hung on to the back of the saddle and whistled to his steed. Peacocks strutted across the palace grounds. Far above, a falcon rode the open sky. The prince had a horse for the princess hidden in a grove of fir trees, where songbirds sang and the boughs surged in the hot winds like the waves of the sea. They could reach that hidden grove by nightfall if they hurried.

I'm not sure if it's a bear ahead or a spruce tree; the outline's blurred. You see, we're above tree line, so there are almost no evergreens here, and where one has managed to cling to the mountain face, its shadow invariably looks like a bear. I unbutton my shirt pocket and take out the monocle my dad once cut from binoculars for me. I use a monocle instead of binoculars because I have a lazy eye—*strabismus* is the real name, I think. It means I can't focus the images from both my eyes into one image. Kind of strange, because my eyes see just fine, but my brain doesn't receive the messages properly. Some people with this condition go cross-eyed. Their weak eye rolls about and wanders until surgery sticks it in place. Others, like me, just slowly lose the ability to see from their bad eye. Mostly I shut that eye when I'm outside and looking out over any distance. I don't even realize I'm doing it, but Dad noticed when I was little. He made me this monocle and a pirate patch for my sixth birthday. Come to think of it, it was the last birthday present he gave me — I don't know what happened to the patch. The real trouble with my eyes, though, is that while I see surfaces all right, I don't have much depth perception. The world is kind of flat for me.

I scan the river bottom ahead of us but can't find the bear. Unfortunately, I can't find the spruce tree either.

The dark spot, whatever it was, is long gone.

I try to remember "The Princess and the Pea" next, but it's hard to concentrate with my heart thumping so fast. Even I know the made-up story can't compete with the possibility of being eaten myself. It's scary here again. I roll up my shirtsleeves and examine the hairs on my arms. They're standing upright.

This is ridiculous. Why did I persuade Mom that I could do this?

It's obvious, even to me, that I can't. It's not too late to go back. But I'll have to figure out a good excuse.

Mom dug her carving chisel into the wood and pressed hard. "I don't want you to go, Rachel." She held the figure close

to the light and gently traced her fingers over its contours. "The answer's no."

I didn't reply.

"I can't help it. It scares me. Anything can happen. You're too young."

"I'll go when I finish school then."

Mom grinned, relieved. "That's years away."

But it wasn't that far away. That's the beauty of correspondence school. We began correspondence school when we lived in the mountains and there were no schools within a hundred miles, but somehow it just worked better for me even when we moved closer to town. I liked getting through my schoolwork in the mornings and having the rest of the day to myself. I crammed the courses I needed to graduate into three years, not four, so I was almost sixteen when I finished high school. When I got my final grades a few months ago, I reminded her I was leaving.

"Just so you know"—she pointed her chisel at my heart— "I don't want you going alone. I can come with you."

"It wouldn't work."

She left the room and neither of us mentioned it for a few days, until one night she dropped a slab of dark chocolate on my pile of gear. "You'll need high-calorie food," she said.

"Sure, Mom," I agreed. I broke off a corner of chocolate and split it between us. "I will come back, you know."

Mom didn't reply. When she doesn't answer, I know she's trying her best not to cry. There are only three things I know for sure about Mom. The rest is kind of up for grabs.

First, she's stoic. When we lived in the bush and ran dogs, I'd see her break trail all day through slush, then help make camp and saw firewood without so much as a cup of tea. Secondly, she's an artist. And lastly, she loves us.

Oh yeah, one more thing: she thinks people are basically kind. When they're not, she doesn't get it.

The only fairy tales I can think of now involve dragons, and the princess usually gets eaten. Or she's saved by the prince, or by a sudden conversion on the dragon's part to vegetarianism. That isn't likely to happen here.

I return to the princess's adventures in the Glass Palace story instead.

The steed rose on his hind legs once, then again, while the prince and the princess hung on, barely breathing. Then, with a toss of his head, the steed galloped across the palace grounds and over the wooden bridge across the moat, through the stone archway and into the green forest beyond, where the princess had always longed to roam.

A nightingale sang from an oak tree by the arch, and a stream gurgled through the moss, flowing into the moat. But the prince and the princess could no longer hear them. They were heading for that hidden grove. They had begun their quest.

A plume of dust trailed behind the horse's hooves and hovered a moment in the still air.

Nah. This isn't a fairy tale: there's a real stream gurgling through the moss. I fling off my pack, unbuckle Brooks's pack and look for wood. Down near the ground, just like Mom taught me. In minutes I'm flat on my stomach with willow twigs heaped in a teepee. My billycan is sloshing beside me, newly filled, and as I blow, smoke drifts from my balled-up newspaper (just for the first couple of days) and flames the wood.

I lean back on my heels and survey my magical kingdom. There are willow clumps and poplars along the creek, and the windswept tundra is dotted with scattered knolls rising from the flat. The trees grow only along the banks, an oasis in an enormous treeless plain. A gust of wind bugles through a boulder outcrop above me. "The Unlikely Forest," I christen the oasis, as it's so unusual to find here.

When I stroll through the trees, picking up dead branches, the air is shadowed and scratchy-sounding with fallen leaves. There were flowers here not long ago; mountain aven and roseroot stalks scrunch underfoot. Only a purple harebell is nosing from the leaf litter, sheltered from the night frosts.

The thing about memorizing is that if I can recite a story whenever I want, then it lives in my head and I can't ever lose it. Fairy tales feel like the source of all true stories to me. All stories I love have at their heart heroism and a quest. If I follow this draw up past the thickets along the creek bank and over the rock slides, I'll come to its headwaters. My first fairy-tale collection feels like the headwater: all other stories flow from it.

Mom kept the tales alive because she repeated them to me. The trouble is that I'm not sure anymore what Mom made up and what really came from the book. And it's started to matter. After Mom finished telling them, I started changing them around too. I couldn't help it. The characters just got sick of being stuck in my head. They felt like victims with destinies out of control. They needed fresh starts and original plot twists.

"That's it," I told Mom. "It's not another planet, you know. I'm just going to walk there and get the book."

Mom carefully placed her chisel in its slot in her wooden case. "Actually," she said, "it is like another planet. It will take you at least two weeks to walk there from the Dempster Highway. That's two weeks mostly across mountain passes with no trail and nobody around if you need help."

"That's okay."

"And for what? You left when you were only six."

"Because it's home."

That's the simple truth.

I'm happy. I'm going home.

I don't remember it much, but I'm going home. That's how it feels.

Of course, there's another story I don't know much about either. The story of how Dad disappeared. All Mom will say is that for a long time he'd been fighting a depression that came and went, that he couldn't completely shake. Because of it, we'd bought a cabin near town that no one wanted, where we still live today. When that didn't help, he went back to our cabin in the bush to be alone for a bit, to try and get better. I remember it was late summer and he didn't even take the dogs. He said he'd be back in a few weeks.

We never saw him or heard from him again.

2

Right on Rolling

I boil water in my billycan while Brooks sleeps by my side, his velvet curtains of ears twitching. Every so often he blinks and shudders, then relaxes into sleep again, snoring. Brooks is one laid-back dog.

I empty out my food bag onto the bank. There's every dried food I could want. Mom and I had peeled and quartered ripe bananas, and dried them with the morel mushrooms we'd picked in an old burn. We spread them, not touching, on window screens hung above the woodstove last summer. As they shrank, I arranged the pieces closer together and added more. We picked wild raspberries and mashed them into leather, which we baked on wax paper in the oven with the door open for several days.

Finally we sliced strips of meat, marinated them and hung them over strings above the stove until they snapped like dead sticks when we broke them in two. Cut, hang, spread—over and over until even Mom looked content when she saw the paper bags bulging in my pack.

"Dry food and butter used to be our staples," said Mom, sticking the butter in freezer bags. "You're leaving in the fall. It shouldn't be hot enough for the butter to melt."

Now I chuck a handful of noodles into the boiling water, break off some cheese and throw in a pinch of dried onions. I drink the broth from the pot, holding it with my shirtsleeves, cross-legged by the scarlet flames. Every couple of minutes I feed in more wood. Willow burns hot and fast, and its smoke streams into my eyes. The fire feels like company.

I don't scan the valley or the mountainsides like I know I should. The creek makes enough noise to cover the sound of anything coming our way. Anyway, with some luck, snoozing Brooks should notice a visitor long before I can.

The noodles smell like willow smoke. Bits of charred wood crunch between my teeth. Dad used to purse his lips and spit into the flames, backward cap across his fore-head, laughing. Suddenly, I'm not hungry anymore. I wake Brooks with the pot shoved under his nose to lick clean, douse the fire with creek water, tie the pot on the outside of my pack and load us up.

I run several steps and leap across our first creek, pack bouncing. Brooks, however, braces himself against the current, wide-legged, and laps noisily. He splashes to the far side, where I wait.

Good thing I've triple-bagged all the gear in his pack. "Let's go," I coax him, hauling on his collar from the shallows. He digs in his paws, whining his way up the cutbank, his pack dragging him back down.

"Don't worry, boy. It'll get lighter," I say just to hear myself talk. And now we're away from the creek and climbing again. I can feel the muscles strain in the back of my thighs. With every step I'm farther away from my family.

And with every step I'm closer to home.

The trail is decades old and overgrown with brush. The sun has moved from my face to my right side. Clouds pile over the peaks like caps slammed onto heads. I hear wind whistling down the gorge ahead. The bushes shake and leaves skitter across my path from the waist-high brush. At least I can see around me. Without proper trees I can see for miles ahead.

Brooks whines deep in his throat and sniffs the wind blowing in our faces. I prop up the shoulder straps of my pack and lean forward to take the weight off for a moment. "Stop it, Brooks," I snap, my voice loud even with the whistling wind. Now the wind is groaning down the shafts of my pack. "Let's go a bit farther," I say. Brooks is standing with his nose high, front paw lifted in a perfect point.

"Our packs are heavy enough," I say. "No hunting on this trip."

But Brooks barks like a bullet spitting from a gun. Then again. The thing about Brooks is that not much riles him up. Mom said once if a burglar broke into our house,

Brooks would just roll over and moan for his belly to be rubbed.

"That's it," I tell him. "Quiet. It's probably a tree." I toss off my pack, scrabble in a pocket for his leash and snap it on. Then I shrug my arms back into the straps, stand and stare.

The dark spot is far ahead and down from the trail on the river bottom, angling across a gravel bar away from us. My monocle stays in my pocket. I don't want to see detail: mouth, claws and hump of muscle rippling above its back. I'll just keep strolling along and make lots of noise.

Trouble is that bears are individuals. Young male bears sometimes *like* noise. They're attracted to it, just like boys. They want to investigate whatever's making that noise. So if a person's walking on a path bears often use, maybe that person should just step aside and not keep hiking along being louder and louder.

Maybe it's not a bear. "You're not even likely to run into a bear," said my sister. "And if you do, they'll probably just run away."

Becky's a dog musher, one of the best for her age. She's put thousands of miles on her dogs and never lost one in harness. In summer she runs them behind an old golf cart that she fixed up.

I stick the monocle to my eye and focus it in. Wrong end—a pat of magnified poop filled with red berries lies smack in the middle of the trail ahead. "Shucks," I tell Brooks, who's pulling at his leash and growling. "Now where do we go?"

Maybe I like fairy tales so much because danger is necessary for heroism. It's not meaningless. When someone calls a story just a fairy tale, they usually mean two things. First, they mean that it's not true. Second, they mean that it has a happy ending. Kind of strange, I think, because fairy tales are brutal. If they end happily, it's only because the characters who remain alive just call the happy part the end. "Whoa!" they shout, waving at the author. "Stop here while we've got a breather. Don't go any farther down this trail."

It's not happy for the princes who've died honorably or their old mothers rattling about in palaces pining for them to gallop home. It's not always so merry for the villagers who've been picked off by the open-jawed, flame-breathing dragons chasing them down the cobblestones. About the best the survivors can do is make up tales of heroism to remember the slaughtered and keep their heads down and hope their own loved ones stay home.

That's a key part of fairy tales: staying home, which is usually way safer than going on a quest. Everyone knows what old maps said at the borders to uncharted lands: *Therein lie dragons*.

"A bear isn't a dragon, you know," I tell Brooks bravely. "Bears are more vegetarians than meat-eaters." I ruffle the fur behind his ears to soothe him. "We're not going back though. I've decided."

Brooks solemnly licks my face. He washes me, concentrating hard on the skin around my mouth. I must smell like food. Or salt. Brooks has a thing about salt.

I take one foot and move it forward. Then the other. I force myself to unfold my arms from my stomach, where I'm hugging myself. I put the monocle up to my eye again in a few minutes, this time scanning above the trail.

The bear is gone. I'm not sure if this is a comfort, as I don't know where or when he'll emerge.

Gray clouds are boiling over the mountain like demented popcorn overflowing a pot. The wind moans. I pull my raincoat and pants from my pack and shrug them on. I'm not camping anywhere near the bear.

The trail climbs and winds across a knoll; raindrops glob together into white wet clumps of slush that slide down my cheeks and collarbone, plastering my hair to my skull even under my hood. The peaks have disappeared. The fog is comforting—or would be if I could quit thinking about being cold. It makes the land seem smaller. I walk and I talk and Brooks trudges along, swaying with each step. I keep the leash snapped between us. I like to feel him there at the end of it, within my reach.

I drink at a creek crossing that is more like a slash through the tundra. The water smells like earth and moss. My rain gear is soaked. The fabric sticks to my wrists and calves. Shivering, I lie on my stomach and put my face flush with the ankle-deep water, moss green from its bed. The current slides fast around a bend. Twigs bob up and down, sweeping the waves. After each gulp, I lift my eyes and scan the far bank. My arms are tightening and loosening, clenching with cold. I have to move.

I stumble on, trying to run until I feel my body relax; then I speed-walk with Brooks trotting at my side.

When the rain has settled to a steady downpour, I stop on open high rocky ground where I can see and be seen. Low-bush cranberries lie like fat, round red apples along their creeping stems of evergreen leaves. Globs of slush are melting as I watch. Even under the snow all winter, cranberry leaves stay green. Easier for the plant not to start every short summer growing new leaves from scratch, I guess.

I get my tent out of a garbage bag, then pull it from its stuff sack and dump out the poles and pegs. It's a one-person mountain tent. A pole threads from side to side across the front and another across the foot end where the ceiling's low. That's it. I stick them in fast but can't peg anything on the thin soil beneath the lichen. I tie the tent ropes to twigs and hope the poles stay balanced. I need to work quickly before the cold makes me clumsy. When I roll back the sleeve of my raincoat, I notice goose bumps like a plucked turkey on my arm. I pull my sleeping bag out of its stuff bag and lay it flat over my blue sleeping pad in the tent. Fingers barely responding, I crawl inside, pulling Brooks after me and shoving him to my feet while I nestle in my bag.

Wherever there's tundra, there's also permafrost. It's a layer of soil and rock that's been frozen year-round for at least two years. The trouble with permafrost is that there's always an active layer above the ice that thaws in the summer and tosses about any structure people try to build over it. That's why it's hard to stick in my poles properly.

"I don't know where he is," Mom kept saying when I was small and I'd ask when he was coming back. "But it's very likely he died in the bush. An accident." I think she wanted to say more, but her voice got small whenever she talked about it. She didn't sound like Mom then, but like someone who was talking from very far away. I didn't understand that when I was a kid, but now I think she was just trying really hard not to cry in front of me. She didn't want me to grow up sad.

Except I knew different.

He said good-bye to me the night before he left. I was tucked in bed after Mom had told me my story. Becky hadn't come to our room yet. Dad slipped in and leaned on the windowsill for a long time. Stars pulsed across the sky, and the first snow lay like icing sugar sifted over the mountains in the distance where he was going. It must have been early fall, just this time of year. He stayed there with his head stuck out the open window for so long that I must have fallen asleep.

He woke me with a hug smelling like snow and the night. "Don't worry, Rachel," he said when I wouldn't let go of his neck. "I'll be back. You just keep right on rolling."

He meant my gymnastics. I rolled right through my child-hood up until he disappeared. Nothing stuck to me.

He took my hands and pried them away from him. He grabbed the baseball cap off his head and shoved it backward onto mine.

"Good night, Rachel," he said. "Sweet dreams."

Then he walked out the door.

What kind of father walks away and doesn't come back? And in the morning, Mom was baking bread as if nothing had happened. "Want a piece to knead?" she asked when I got up.

"Is he gone?" I answered. He must have slipped out when I was asleep. I should have stayed awake so I could stop him.

"We'll put some buns and a loaf in the freezer," said Mom, nodding. "Dad can eat it when he comes back."

I climbed on the chair beside her and made buns like faces, with raisins for eyes and blueberries in a circle for mouths. Every mouth was scowling. The dough was greasy under my fingers.

"How many sleeps until he comes back?" I asked her.

"He's not feeling well. He feels better in the mountains," she said. "He's always been like that."

She hadn't even looked directly at me. Obviously Mom didn't know when Dad was coming back.

Every morning I checked the freezer for my bag of buns. One morning it was gone.

But Dad hadn't come home.

I quit rolling right around then. I wasn't into somersaults anymore or walking on my hands. I walked on stilts that had rigid boots permanently attached right to the crosspiece. All I had to do was step into them and shove off and I'd be hovering over everyone else. I also began juggling seriously. I juggled *anything I could find. I picked up apples or potatoes from the root cellar or even stones from the forest. I'd practice for hours until the light dimmed. Of course, regular life must have gone on then. I did schoolwork and ate meals, but juggling relaxed me. It made me forget that Dad was gone. I had to concentrate on the balls.*

Sometimes I think I picked juggling because of the challenge. Without depth perception I had to kind of feel for the balls. Maybe I wouldn't have tried it if I hadn't listened to a story tape about Beethoven. I couldn't get over that he'd composed symphonies even though he was deaf.

In the evenings, I memorized fairy tales. I'd done it back before I could even read. I'd memorized picturebooks that Mom and Dad read to me and recited the words while I turned the pages. Then in the toboggan, watching the butts of our dogs hunched over in their harnesses, I'd have something to do that didn't freeze my fingers like turning pages did.

My fingers, stuck in my armpits, are tingling. I shake them over the sleeping bag for a minute and stick them back in to thaw some more.

Becky says that people who don't have a written language memorize their histories instead. Anthropologists are amazed at the accuracy of their accounts, going back sometimes for hundreds of years. I, however, wasn't aiming for truth. At least not until recently.

Only the far corners of my bag are still frigid. I explore them with my feet, stretching so that my own heat spreads to the corners. Time to tell Brooks a story.

And so the princess traveled on with the merry prince and their loyal steeds. They rode through open glades and splashed through pebbled creeks and climbed the steep faces of mighty mountains. The wind was fresh on their faces, the air was crisp and bright in a late summer sky, and their hearts were full of wonder as they trotted across this new and lovely land, searching for a mythical lake that was rumored to be the source of all true stories.

I've been dozing like a baby with my legs drawn up to my stomach and my arms wrapped around my waist. I'm almost warm. I poke my head out into the growing darkness. The sky has blown clear, and stars stretch with a zillion pulses of faraway light from one side of the valley to the other.

I haven't wrapped up my camp for the night, I realize. I need to be ready in case a bear comes sniffing around.

The memory of being cold is so recent that it sets me vibrating again at the thought of the night air. I climb out on my stomach and unpack my wool hat, my flashlight, my bear spray and a pen-shaped device called a bear banger.

I screw one orange cap of gunpowder into its end and carry three more into my tent. Lying down again, I put my hat on my head and use my sweater for a pillow. I need to arrange my defenses where I can find them by feel in the dark. I prop up my empty boot and drop everything into it. I could find it by smell as well. My boots smell like moss. All I have to do with the bear banger is pull back one end, and the gunpowder will explode into the sky like a firecracker.

Brooks crawls up and lies on me, legs spread like a roasting chicken. Claustrophobic, I kick him off and he curls against the wall, making it shake. I shove him back to my feet and, feeling guilty, sit up to scratch his warm belly for a moment, my sleeping bag bunched about my waist. He moans, content. Eyes closing, I curl up again, relaxed and warm.

My pack is still too close if a hungry bear wanders past.

I crawl out yet again.

I drop my pack close enough that I'll see a bear coming to investigate, but not so close he feels compelled to investigate me too. Unfortunately, there are no trees here so I can't sling it over a high branch.

Back in the tent, I'm wide awake. My stomach rumbles and then twists. I didn't eat enough, I know. I mound my sweater-pillow underneath me and stare at the roof sagging above my head. I unzip the outer door so I can see a crack into the night. I want to be able to run out if I need to, not fumble with the zippers of the screen and the nylon doors. I fall asleep with one fist curved around the toe of my boot. Brooks lies with his head on my stomach and snores.

My stomach growls like a bear in the night.

3

So What Is a Bear?

Grizzly, grizzle us,
Ursus horribilis,
Moonlight dribble us,
You can't get me!

Not bad, I think. When I'm half awake, poems some-times pop into my head. I'm a better sleeping poet than an awake one. I think of my mind as a long corridor with rooms opening off it. The poem-making room is sunny, with bright yellow walls and tall skinny windows letting in mountain views. Unfortunately, I can knock on the door in the day, but only in the early morning does it swing open.

I lie in my bag with the low morning sun on my tent walls and floor, bathing me in warmth. *Ursus horribilis* used to be the Latin name for grizzly bear. Brooks yawns and stretches and the tent shakes. I stick my head out without getting out of my bag. The moon is sinking below a plug of rock at the top of some no-name peak. The upper mountain faces are rosy and fresh from the rising sun. Brooks licks my face at the same moment I open my mouth to speak. Gross!

I'm happy. It isn't dark anymore, and I don't have to say good-bye to anyone today. As well, it's completely up to me what I do with my day.

An hour later the sunshine has moved down from the peaks and is shining on the willows. White-crowned sparrows flash above me from bush to bush. My first choice, which is to stay in bed, won't work. To do that, I'd need someone to build the fire for me and cook my breakfast.

I fling open the tent door and hop out, still in my sleeping bag, collecting dry twigs in the clumps of bushes. I don't step out of my bag until the little fire is blazing and spitting sparks into the sunshine. I like the sound the sparks make as they pop and fly away.

Brooks is sniffing down the trail, nose to ground. Brooks *always* has his nose on the ground unless a large mammal like a bear, wolf, moose or caribou is close. In that case, it's up in the air and he's talking away—kind of a cross between a yip and a drawn-out moan.

***

"What could have happened to him, Mom?" I asked her once when he'd been gone a few years.

Mom only talked about Dad's good side to me. She figured if I only remembered the happy times, then I wouldn't be traumatized.

From the way she talked, I thought Dad was her hero, not her husband.

"I don't know," she said, which was her usual answer. "You want me to tell you but I can't. I don't know." Already her voice had that faraway sound to it that scared me into not asking anymore. She didn't sound like the Mom I loved then. She sounded like she was walking away too.

"A bear could have got him," said Becky helpfully from the couch, where she was sewing a chewed-up dog harness. "Or he could have fallen through the ice." Sharp cheekbones, masses of curly black hair, a gymnast's strong thin body and energy crackling from her like a live wire: Becky is beautiful and couldn't care less.

"It was fall," I snapped. "The river wasn't frozen yet. Honestly."

"Okay," said my sister. "You know what I mean. It could have been the river or breaking a leg when he was up sheep hunting. Maybe he surprised a bear when he was coming home. Why does it matter how it happened? He's gone."

Maybe he isn't gone. That's the thing. Maybe he's wandering around the mountains somewhere and doesn't think he should come home. Maybe he thinks we're happier without him, and he's living on caribou meat and berries and wild pea roots and lichen, boiled and drained and boiled again until he can digest it. He's probably got a few hooks for fishing waist-high in the current, and he's snapped off a green willow pole and is drying the fish for winter.

If bears come around to take their share, he probably just keeps on with whatever he's doing, ignores them. 'Cause he wouldn't be scared. He wouldn't be scared because he wouldn't really care if the bear ate him too. He'd think he wasn't worth anything, just because he never came home.

Grizzlies come in different colors. They can be yellow, brown and even black, and black bears can be brown. One quarter of the world's population of grizzlies lives in the Yukon. They're smaller than other grizzlies because the land isn't so productive, and they roam a bigger range. Grizzlies have evolved naturally to live above the tree line; black bears live in the forest. That's why black bears are better at climbing trees, but it's also why I'm more comfortable seeing them around. They're used to melting into the forest or climbing up a tree. Grizzlies are more likely to stand their ground if you surprise them.

Mom told me that if you treat bears with respect, they'll respect you back. What's she talking about? Why would a bear feel anything for me but minor irritation? *Oh, not her again*, it probably thinks, *wandering around with that smelly dog*.

Becky's latest litter of sled-dog puppies was rampaging about the room one night shortly before I left. "I love fairy tales too," *she pronounced, "but I know they're not real."*

I was sprawled mostly on the couch—feet up, head on the floor—reading Hansel and Gretel. *"So do I," I snapped.*

Two wooly pups were tugging at strands of my hair, pulling and growling, bracing themselves for the kill. Becky lay on her back holding a third puppy over her face, kissing his nose.

"Gross!" She bolted upright, wiping her cheeks.

Released, her pup joined the brave attack on my hair. Becky actually spat on the floor. "He peed on my face," she muttered when she could speak.

But she's right. I do think fairy tales are, if not exactly real, at least true. They contain truth in them somewhere. I've thought about this for a long time, maybe since before I was old enough to be able to express my thoughts. Perhaps long ago, when people began telling those stories, there wasn't a difference between wind and spirits, bears and power. At least not to them.

Sometimes I can almost see early storytellers crouched under the stars around a fire, drawing stories from the natural world they knew, like I might draw a bucket of water from a mountain pond.

I think about this a lot. See, not only do we not believe anymore that bears, for example, are power, but we mostly don't have a clue what an actual bear is. What is his favorite berry? Where does he sleep? What does he like to smell on the warm spring breeze? Does he miss his mom when he moves away? We don't have any idea what it means to be a bear, and we don't truly believe that a bear contains spiritual power, so what on earth is the point of a bear in a story?

Once I asked Mom if she thought bears had emotions like people, if they ever got lonely.

She was sketching cross-legged under a tree, her chisels beside her and the slab of wood flat on the ground. Sometimes Mom likes to get down the bones of a sketch first, then transfer it to a slab of wood. She copies the sketch on the wood first, then carves the outline and burns the picture to the right shade. To the side, a bonfire blazed in a ring of stones. Mom needed the heat for her hands.

"Maybe wolves get lonely," she said, glancing up at me. "They're social animals. But bears? I don't know. They live with their mother first and then sometimes den with a sibling for the first winter after she runs them off. When they leave their sibling, the males live alone." She brushed her hair off her forehead, leaving a streak of charcoal. "I think all animals have feelings, but I can't imagine what they're like because I can't imagine what they want."

Mom looks like an older version of Becky—a bit cleaner and neater but the general effect of careless beauty is the same. Logs collapsed into the flames and settled, shooting sparks.

Mom was drawing a great horned owl in a cottonwood tree. The fact that the owl had flown away days earlier was irrelevant. In Mom's eye he was perched in the high bare branches just through the haze of her campfire smoke.

"Okay, Brooks," I say, sifting through my food bag. "You can't walk all day if you haven't eaten anything." I scoop out a cup of dry dog food for his breakfast and pour it on a bit of tinfoil on the ground. I don't want any to touch the ground or its smell might linger there.

Brooks crunches slowly, with great pleasure and concentration, and then lies on his stomach, tail sweeping the ground, in begging position. His sad eyes lock onto mine and he nuzzles my knees with his nose.

"Greasy oats?" I suggest. I mix oats and brown sugar and butter and dry berries with water in my pot and let it boil for a few minutes. I can hear the boiling even above the noise of the creek. A white-crowned sparrow calls from a willow clump. The sun shines gently on my skin and I eat half the pot and give the rest to Brooks. Saves on washing dishes when he licks out the pot.

Before we leave, I take out three juggling balls and stand on the creek bank. Basic juggling is called a cascade because the balls rise up the center and flow down the outside again and again. It's the most relaxing hobby in the world. I whistle and juggle until I remember the marmots.

Grizzlies dig out TONS of rocks just to get at marmots in their underground burrows. And guess how the father marmot sounds the alarm. He whistles! So if you don't go out of your way to associate your presence with food, grizzlies will probably leave you alone. If you do something dumb, like whistle, there may be consequences.

The word *probably* isn't all that comforting when I'm alone.

The balls are smooth and warm on the palms of my hands, and the tundra goes on forever. The white-crowned sparrow calls six notes. "Give me a clue for you," I chant so I can remember its song, ascending and then descending at the end.

Brooks yawns and I put away the balls; then I pack and shoulder my load. I'm achier than yesterday. My neck cracks when I move it. I walk with my hand under a shoulder strap to ease the pressure. I don't want to leave my camp. Already it feels so safe; it feels like my home. Every time I light a campfire, I make a new home. In a few years, I'll have the whole watershed feeling like my backyard.

The sky is blue and blazing with heat. The bushes come alive with swarming blackflies. I don't have a watch. It's hard to walk forward because I'm nervous. The valley curves to the right so the place where my family left me will disappear from sight soon. I won't be able to turn around to see where the road lies anymore. I'll have to figure out which pass to go through when I want to go back. Stupid, I know. I mean, I'm following a trail at this point.

But when I walk a few paces off the trail, I see no trace of anything but tundra. It's weird that people take up so little physical and so much mental space. Blink and they're gone, and yet after he disappeared, my dad lived forever scrambled in my brain. I trot back to the trail and keep moving.

Midday means lunch, but I don't want any. I perch on my pack and grab chocolate chunks from Brooks's load. Brooks scrapes his pack at my legs, so I lift it off. He chases his tail a minute in delight, ears flapping like an elephant's. I love chocolate. Mom and Becky and I keep good chocolate in the cupboard at all times. I nibble to make it last.

Brooks stares mournfully into my eyes from two inches away, begging, but I know dogs can't digest chocolate and it would just make him sick. I cradle his head on my lap and play with his floppy ears instead. Far away, a line of willow shows where a creek crosses the trail. "We'll have supper there," I tell him.

Brooks leaps up and barks. My heart bangs in my chest. Panic floods through me before I can even see what he's barking at.

Two bull caribou saunter a hundred feet away, their antlers bobbing as they move. They circle around, heads tossed high so they're facing downwind. Strips of bloody velvet hang from the branches of their antlers—time for them to shed. Only when they're positioned to catch our scent do they bolt.

The chunk of chocolate in my hand is stabbed with my teeth marks. Chocolate is smeared over my fingers. I don't want it anymore. What is my problem?

"Let's go, Brooks," I whisper, and we do.

Hansel and Gretel outsmarted the witch who'd locked them in the cottage in the forest. They stuck a chicken bone through the bars of their cage to trick her. "Too skinny!" cried the witch and heaped on the rations.

Out here, everything eats or is eaten by something else. The vegetarians are eaten by the carnivores. The predators get kicked in the ribs by moose or caribou and hole up under the overturned roots of a cottonwood tree to lick their wounds and eventually die. What's it like to die? Can it be peaceful lying under the sky in pain while, far off on the horizon, peaks grow smaller because of the Earth's curve? Wolves sometimes eat their prey alive, Dad told me. What does an animal think about when it knows it's going to die? Dad loved to hunt. I remember walking beside him. It must have been in the valley by the cabin, because I can see big spruce trees in my mind and they only grow like that along the river-valley bottoms. I remember an explosion and a bull moose running across a gravel bar before us and then falling first to its knees and then onto its side. The gravel bar was ribboned with sunshine. Dad and I walked up to the moose's mountainous side and waited quietly a minute. I wanted to hold his hand, but I was scared of his gun.

The moose's front legs kicked. Then it lay still. Not a sound.

"Poor moose," I mumbled.

"Don't tell me that bothers you," he laughed.

So I didn't tell him.

But of course it did.

In the afternoon the sun gets very hot, and no-see-ums swarm on my eyelids and lips and behind my ears. They burrow underneath my hair and crawl on my sweaty neck. I keep hunching forward with my hands under my pack's shoulder straps to give myself a moment's break from its weight. Then I let go to swat the bugs.

Sometimes the trail divides, and I'm not sure which fork to take. So far, the forks have come back together. But what if they don't? I start breaking off dry willows and placing them on the ground in the shape of arrows pointing in the direction I've come from. Then I can retrace my steps if I need to return.

I walk, singing a bit just to hear myself. The wind comes up like it did yesterday, and clouds sail above the peaks and blanket the valley I'm walking through. I pull on extra clothes and keep walking. Supper is cold food: dry meat and cheese and water straight from a creek.

While I rest, my mind hops ahead, droning with nerves like the blackflies slithering along my skin.

At first we called Dad on an evening "sched" Mom had set up with him. Often we heard only static. Once we heard his voice calling for a radio check very faintly.

"This is Caribou Creek on a radio check," he repeated, his voice as low as possible to carry. "Can anybody copy?"

"This is Caribou Creek portable," we shouted into the microphone, louder and louder, taking it in turn, each one convinced our voice would be the one to reach him. "We can copy but it's faint."

No reply.

Then came days when we could hear other people with radios around the territory. But no Dad. Northern lights can interfere with radio signals. At first we thought there was just a particularly strong solar storm in the atmosphere.

The days turned to weeks.

"Why didn't you call the police earlier to search?" I heard Becky ask Mom once.

"Because I didn't know his plans," she said. "He didn't even know them. So I didn't know if he was missing until it was way too late."

✳

I scrub the blackflies from the corners of my eyes. Surely I must remember more from before he left. I don't try to control where my thoughts land. I just keep them in the air before the memory flies away.

✳

I was lying in bed, one thin wall from the kitchen, listening to Mom and Dad talk when they thought I couldn't hear.

I was small, and there was a glass of water by my bed. Moonlight spilled through my window onto my pillow and blankets. I wasn't allowed to read anymore and I was restless. I pretended I was in the desert, and I didn't know when I'd be rescued. A sip of water had to last me all day in the searing heat. My camels lay on the sand...

"I need to get my head together," Dad said. "I need to be alone."

"Please don't go. I can't stand it if you go."

Dad's voice rasped. "I can't help you."

I wondered how many days it would take me to die of thirst in the desert.

Months later the police launched a search with two heli-copters. When I wondered why we were staying with neighbors for the day, Becky said Mom was worried. Nobody was all that surprised that he had disappeared, it seemed. Only I believed he was coming back.

Mom was dropped off at the cabin on that first flight. An officer went with her. She said years later that it felt like Dad had just walked out the door, expecting to return. His red lumberjack shirt was on the back of his chair, smelling like sweat, smoke and tobacco. Nothing was put away. She lugged food and gear up the ladder to the cache and hunted for a note.

While she was at the cabin, the police helicopter searched, throbbing up and down the valley and especially along the river's banks where his body might be bobbing in an eddy. Caribou must have bolted. Grayling must have held themselves motionless with noses pressed against the current, waiting for the sky to grow still.

They flew back to the cabin once more after Mom came back, and that time they looked farther away. I remember them coming to the door of our place near town afterward.

I was looking out the window, waiting for Dad like I did every day back then, and instead saw two cops cut across the front yard and up the steps. They were dressed in red uniforms with black stripes down their pant legs. I swung open the door, with Mom and Becky right behind me. Mom didn't ask them to come in. I guess she didn't want to talk with them longer than she had to. She tried to shoo us back inside, but we only went as far as the doorway and listened, huddled together.

"Where will you search next?" she said.

The cops looked at each other. "The search has been called off. If something happened to him, it's too late," one said finally. "I'm sorry. We have no idea how long he meant to be gone or where he planned to go. You don't really even know if he's actually still in the bush. He's been out there for months. And he knows that country. It's not like he would have got lost."

Becky broke away from the doorway and bolted across the yard. She spent the rest of the day curled up under the house with her knees drawn up to her chest and her head down. I know because I found her. Mom tried to coax her out when she got rid of the cops, but couldn't. Eventually I crawled in with a plate of stew and lay on my stomach beside her while she ate. Neither of us said a word. I remember being relieved that she ate.

At bedtime she emerged and let Mom hold her. Only years later did I realize that Mom hadn't reacted much at all. Whatever sorrow crashed over her that day, she hugged it to herself. I guess she didn't have much choice if she wanted us to have a normal life. There was no one there to hold her.

At first, Mom just told me she didn't know what had happened. She came in to my room every night and asked me what story I wanted and then she told it to me.

One night I told her that I didn't like the ending.

She laughed and kissed my cheek. "Then change it," she said. "I'll tell you any ending you like."

"But doesn't it have to be the true one?" I asked.

"No, silly," said Mom. "They're all made up, however they end."

That's when I started memorizing on purpose. I asked for fairy-tale collections every birthday, every Christmas. Mom didn't have to tell me stories anymore. She'd given me my own.

4

A Grizzled Bear

That night I camp again by a creek with my pack visible through some low willows, but not too close. I put up my tent in the last of the light and juggle on the creek bank with Brooks on his haunches, mouth gaping like a fish, staring at the flowing balls. I add the fourth ball at the end. I toss eighteen passes in reverse cascade before I drop one in his mouth. Cool. I like it. Brooks sits, tail sweeping, until I call him for the ball.

It's strange with juggling. Because I'm focused so much on the balls, everything else both slips away and comes clearer when I'm done. After I've juggled I have incredible concentration for a few hours. The light pats the top of the far mountains and then is gone. I leave bear spray, flashlight and bangers in my boot again for easy reach. Brooks snuggles at my side, and I sleep in my sweater so I can keep my arm out of the bag, wrapped around his warm chest. I want to feel him breathe.

You'd think the older I get, the less I'd worry about the past. But it's just the opposite. It's like Dad lives in my head, calling me. His voice isn't sad or angry; it is simply there every morning when I tumble out of my dreams. Trouble is, I like it. His voice is all I have left of him, and once I'm fully awake each morning, even that's gone.

I haven't seen the cabin since I was a little girl. When we left because Dad was depressed, we thought it would just be for a little while and then we'd come back. My books, including the Irish fairy tales, must be in the cache with the remains of our gear. There should even be some food that's still edible, staples like flour and rice. As far as I know, no one's gone back there since Mom and the cops searched while the helicopter hovered over the valley. At first I concentrated hard on forgetting the years we lived there. When a memory popped up, I forced it to fly instantly up and away, like a spark from a fire.

A picture flashes into my head of the clearing with moonlight sliding over the surface of the river out my window and then lighting the wall of spruce trees and the mountain rising beyond.

Cabin. River. Forest and mountain, I think. *Moonlight covers it all*. I crack the tent zipper again and leave it open for easy exiting if I need to. The bugs have all gone to bed. Brooks snores at my side. The tundra is completely still, no wind sweeping the buckbrush, no songbirds flitting between the shrubs. Only at night can we see ourselves in context, I realize, one planet moving amid countless pricks of light, the familiar daytime sky peeled away like a blanket.

The next thing I know, it's morning.

Brooks is growling outside the tent.

Terror leaps up and slams into me. I'm breathing way too fast, gasping, muscles contracting and loosening. "Calm," I whisper, holding my own shaking body. I visualize the cabin and clearing bathed in sunlight. The memory settles like a ball, warm in the cup of my hand. I wrap my arms tighter around my chest.

Then he's barking in ugly bursts like a shotgun in the silence. I want to curl on my side inside the sleeping bag. I want to shut my eyes and hug myself. Brooks will take care of whatever's out there. I count to ten. Brooks sounds frantic.

I crawl out through the screen door on my belly.

What looks like a giant skunk stands by my pack. Maybe it is one, kind of like the giant beavers who wandered around here during the last ice age. I close my eyes and open them again—the creature's still there, and I can see it's not a skunk. Wind murmurs through the bushes bordering the trail, soft and silvery like faraway surf.

It has to be a bear.

The animal is black with a yellow stripe glinting like wet gold in the early sun. The stripe begins on the back of its head and flows along its humped grizzly back to its tail. The brush about him glistens with dew. Hair is rising all over my body; I've never seen anything like it.

Brooks simply stands, unmoving, his left front leg lifted, vomiting barks. The fur on *his* back bristles like porcupine quills.

The bear yawns. Glancing toward us, he flips my pack over with his paws. He tosses it once in the air and darts a glance at me again. Several times he looks away and back, as if I'm of no importance.

Unfortunately, I know that's how bears act when they're stressed.

The pack thuds closer to him, and the bear hooks it with a paw. He looks like Brooks playing with a ball, the hump behind his shoulders rippling as he moves. The bear heaves himself up and stands on his back legs, woofing.

"Hey, bear," I say. Blood is pulsing in my ears like a waterfall. The ground is cold beneath my sock feet. I'm holding my boot full of defenses. Wind gusts. A tide of terror curls over me like a monster wave poised to crash. I can feel it ripping through my body, right into my feet and hands. My whole body wants to run.

The bear dangles his short arms in front of his chest and waves his head back and forth. He smells like meat, must have been chewing on a carcass somewhere. My stomach turns over.

"Hey, bear," I repeat, more loudly, my hands above my head to make myself bigger. My voice surges in my ears like breaking surf. My boot is tight in one hand. I am like a mother clutching a drowning child in the backwash.

Brooks doesn't move.

The bear sits.

"Good dog, Brooks," I whisper to comfort myself.

The bear gets back on all fours, pokes at the pack with his snout and wanders slowly off. I can see his yellow stripe moving clearly above the brush.

I stand very still and listen to my heart.

What do I do now?

Should I scare him with the banger?

Or let him be, relieved he's in retreat?

Slowly, birds emerge and flicker between the bushes: two redheaded tree sparrows with a dark dot on their breasts like a target. Almost out of sight, a cow moose and calf amble through the willows and disappear into a draw.

I take my tent down and stuff my pack. I keep Brooks tied to a bush until I start to walk off down the trail, singing my head off. The words sound strange. I cover my jaw with my hand: it's trembling. I'll eat breakfast later, I think, when I've found somewhere I can see in all directions. Right now I need to move. My hands are shaking too. The leash connecting me to Brooks vibrates like a fishing pole.

Mom said she'd come in a month. Check on me is what she meant. I don't want her to. I don't want any limits.

I want to go back to our cabin and look for Dad on my own. I want to lie in my childhood bed by candlelight and read my fairy-tale book and cook my own meals and be free.

Tonight I'll stay awake all night. I'll keep walking until I'm out of the pass and down in the spruce trees again.

I can collect enough wood there to keep a fire going all night. I'll break off a dead pole and sleep in the open beside the fire with the pole beside me. If the bear comes back, I'll stick one end in the flames and hold it out.

Nah, I think, I'm a juggler. I can juggle fire. I'll stick three poles in the fire, and I'll swing them all. The poles will *whoosh* with flame, bright in the dark air, and I'll sing along.

The air's different today: colder. I walk for miles with Brooks swaying at my side, blackflies lifting in the breeze and sunshine falling on my left cheek.

There's no sign of the bear, no tracks or droppings. Once a black fox stands on a knoll and looks curiously at us before trotting up a draw. Another time, I count eleven caribou cows crossing an open plain before us, calves racing on stilt legs among them. Several Dall sheep bed down in the sunshine on rocky outcrops far above the trail, like splatters of white cream against the stone.

There was never a moment when I crossed the line between knowing Dad would come home and doubting it. As time went

on, it seemed less and less likely to Mom and Becky, that was all. In the beginning, we all pictured him clearly. I still have his baseball cap in a drawer, our family picture by my bed. In the picture, our dogs are harnessed with the sled still hooked to a tree, and Dad is cross-legged in front of the packed sled. Becky and I are tucked into the shelter of his arms. Mom has slid into the corner of the frame, laughing, after propping up the camera.

Even after we got electricity in town, we still lit kerosene lights when we went to bed. The light is soft and yellow enough to leave corners shadowed. Mine hung on a nail hammered into the log wall above my bed. When I was asleep, Mom came in and blew into the top of the globe to snuff out the wick. I woke for a moment to the smell of the kerosene and Mom bending quietly to kiss me good night.

That's how I thought of Dad, quietly and peacefully blown out. Then Mom kissing him good night.

"He would have come back if he could," she repeated, month after month, then year after year. "He loved us. And he'd want you to grow up happy."

But she never met my eyes when she said this. And her voice was quiet and slow as if she spoke from far away.

"What was he like?" I'd bug her when my memories began to fade. "Did he like being alone? Did he juggle? Or tell jokes? What did he like to eat?"

At first, Mom would weave stories of Dad into our nightly fairy tales. "The princess's father," she might say, sitting on the edge of my bed, "was a famous woodsman. He could talk with birds and all the creatures of the forest. Every morning he would take up his ax and go into the forest to cut trees. Then one morning when the dew was still on the grass, everything changed in a single moment."

But after she left my room, I lay alone and reworked the ending in my head. "And the woodcutter never returned," I might say, "and the princess grew up alone in the hut at the edge of the forest, waiting for a glimpse of him through the trees. Day after day, she waited. The seasons passed. Snow came and went, but her father did not return. 'Daddy,' she used to shout when nobody could hear her. All the longing of the waiting years was in her voice. 'Daddy!'"

"Look," said Becky one day when she'd had enough of my questions. "Pick something that might have happened to him and tell yourself that's how he died. Most likely he drowned. He was probably crossing a river and stepped into a deep spot and the current took him away."

"Could he swim?" I asked.

"Actually," said Becky, "he could, but not too well. That isn't the point." She stood, stretched and yawned, dainty and tough in her red wool pants, lumberjack shirt and cloud of long black hair. Her massive wheel dog, Chili, uncurled himself from behind the stove and went to her, happy for a run.

"Want to come with me and the dogs tomorrow? I need some weight."

"What is your point?" I asked, my juggling balls cradled against my chest.

She bent down to scratch Chili's ears. "That you realize he's dead. That you get a life."

This was interesting. Why did she think I hadn't realized it? Unless, of course, it wasn't really true.

I threw the balls up so the outside balls met at the top of the arc and crossed over. I wasn't talking with her anymore about Dad dying. "Juggling's simple," I told her. "One day I could teach you too."

Becky hugged me. She put her arms around my shoulders. "Come with us. I'll teach you what Dad showed me about running dogs."

"Can't," I said. "I'm juggling."

Around suppertime I walk past the perfect spot for a fire, but I don't even hesitate. I'm not hungry yet.

After another hour, I realize that if I don't stop to eat soon, I'll have to boil supper where I camp. I don't want cooking smells around my tent tonight.

I heap twigs in a teepee, stretch out on my stomach and light a fire. White flames lick along the wood and crackle cheerfully into the still, clear sky. The weather sure changes fast in these mountains. Brooks lies down. I unbuckle his pack, and he rolls happily on the moss and wades into the creek up to his chest. The current breaks around him and flows on past a gravel bar. Brooks growls and snaps up mouthfuls of water, then splashes back to shore.

I fill my pot and boil a stew with dry meat and vegetables and rice. It's not bad, although all the broth

boils away. I add a dollop of butter and eat it with a stick—
I've lost my spoon somewhere. So far I haven't eaten much
on this trip. Not enough. Dad was like that, I think. Mom
said that he'd walk for a day and take only a package of
soup to boil at night.

I force myself to eat until my stomach feels tight for
once and give the leftovers to Brooks. I wash out the pot
with hot water to get rid of food smells, tie it to the outside
of my pack and wander on. My pants are hanging on me.
I have to keep hitching them up. The trail is heading
downhill now. Tomorrow I should be in the river valley.
Tomorrow we'll walk through the shadows of trees.

Before I go to sleep, I try to decide what I'll dream.
Mom told me that she could do it. She just figures it out
before she's asleep, and, mostly, whatever she picks will
show up in her dreams. No bears, I chant to myself. No
bears in my camp. No bears in my dreams. I'm half asleep
when I realize what I *do* want is to dream about Dad.

That night, I dream I'm at the cabin and he's sitting in
the kitchen by the woodstove, whittling a spoon. "Here,"
he says, laughing as he holds it out to me. "Take it. It will
help you eat."

I wake up in the dark, sweating, the wind moaning over
the tundra again. It was his voice that I remember now.
I haven't heard it since I was a little kid. Even more clearly,
I can hear his laugh. It makes me want to bury my face in
his sweater. I can smell the wood smoke from the stove
and I can still smell him, after all these years.

Mom never told us there was a letter. Not for years. When she went to search for him after he disappeared, she'd found no clues at all. The letter was stuck in the back of a drawer in our house in town.

She finally showed it to us. And that's why I'm here.

5

Imposing Order

"At least," said Becky, "we know he died happy. He was out where he wanted to be."

We were standing by the woodstove with our hands out to the heat, Mom carving at her worktable beside us. Becky was stirring a five-gallon tin bucket of meat scraps and oil and grain for her team. Our cabin always smelled like wood smoke and Becky's dog food.

"But we don't really know if he's dead," I said, puzzled. I backed away from the heat and picked up my juggling clubs. They're shaped like gaudy bowling pins and they spin when you throw them. If you get really good, you can spin two or three clubs.

It was winter and the northern lights danced like charmed snakes across the sky. The clubs were awkward. You shouldn't impose your own order on the objects being juggled, I'd read.

Clubs and balls have their own patterns, different each time
you throw them. A cup of water can be absorbed back into
a stream. Not so in juggling. A lost catch is gone forever.
Let it go.

"Of course we do," said Mom, as always.

I had four clubs in the air so I couldn't break concentration.
When I don't focus, the balls or clubs begin to drift away from
me and I have to chase them. Good jugglers should be able to
stand completely still with their feet rooted. Only their lower
arms and wrists should move. If a juggler moves forward even
an inch, the balls or clubs will continue to creep forward. Soon
they will be out of reach. Novices juggle with a wall in front of
them to combat drift.

"Prove it," I said. I'd never have spoken if I hadn't been
so focused. All those years, I'd never asked her to prove
anything.

Mom came into my room with the letter when I was
almost asleep. She handed it to me and stood by the window,
looking out at the bowl of stars and distant mountains.

"I'm sorry," I read. "I'm no good to you anymore. But I loved
each of you. I hope you remember that."

I let the letter drop onto my blankets and clutched
my stomach.

"Why didn't you show it to me before?"

"Because it was for me," she said. "And I didn't want you
to know that he'd killed himself. But you need to understand
he's dead."

I shocked us both by laughing. "But it doesn't say that at all,"

I sputtered. "It only says he's sorry. He would never kill himself. He told me he'd come home."

Mom sat at the bottom of my bed. "The sad part for me," she said, looking directly at me, "is that it's possible for you to choose not to live your life properly. You really can choose to wait for him all your life if that's what you want to do. But it would be a bloody waste."

The next day I started cutting up food to dry: peel and cut, peel and cut. I took the screen windows off the shed and hammered spikes above the woodstove to rest the racks on. It was all a misunderstanding, I realized. All these years and no one had bothered to search again. I put my hand tightly over my mouth.

He'd shoved his baseball cap on my head. "I'll be back," he told me, turning at the door to wave. And yet in the letter he said he wasn't any good to us.

There's a moment in the cascade when I feel the balls will drop past my outstretched hands and bounce on the floor, out of my control.

"Doesn't it get boring," asked Becky, "doing the same thing again and again?"

But it doesn't. When the balls leave my hands there's no guarantee they'll return. Sometimes I let them bounce: one, two, three, and catch them with a flourish as if that had been my plan all along.

"You're not going," repeated Mom every day, suddenly looking old amidst a heap of wood shavings. She looked absent, like she'd looked in the first years after Dad disappeared.

I hugged her then. I didn't quite know how to tell her that I didn't care what she wanted anymore. And I wanted to care.

The only way that would happen was for me to go back to the cabin and see for myself.

Alone.

6

Building on Permafrost

The next day, islands of dark green forest float on the sea of tundra. Tundra comes from a Finnish word meaning treeless plain. The isolated patches of alpine trees that grow at the border of forest and tundra are called *krumholz*. Becky taught me that. I glimpse trees first from the top of a little bump of a hill studded with boulders. When the trail wanders down again, I lose sight of them until, after a few miles of flat steady walking, the trail begins to slope gradually downhill. The river line gleams to the left. Creeks flow out to join it from each fold in the mountains.

When I reach the first spruce clump, I see that there is a parent tree inside a circle of smaller trees: clones sprouted from the original tree's branches, which must have sunk into the moss and leaf litter under heavy snows some long-ago winter. Black spruce reproduces this way in the Far North; so do trembling aspen. Aspen seeds die so fast when they leave the parent tree and need such specific conditions to germinate that they rarely travel up here. You can tell clones because they're all somehow still connected. In the fall, whole hillsides will change color, patch by patch, clone by clone. In the spring, the clones leaf up together too. It's pretty weird how plants and animals adapt simply to survive on the cold dark tundra. You'd think they'd just not bother.

The trunks are wind-blasted and twisted. I snap off a fistful of twigs drooping with old-man's beard and stuff the lacy, green-black lichen in a pocket of my pack to light my supper fire. I walk on, crushing spruce cones between my fingers and breathing in the smell before I toss them away. Black spruce cones often stay on the tree for many years unless a forest fire comes along to force them open. I'll just help these along.

As I walk, the distant glints become silvery river bends. Huge cottonwoods with bare upflung arms grow on the banks beside tangled clumps of head-high willow and alder. Spruce are spaced in open woods farther back. Ptarmigan will be flocking now, socializing after a busy summer of raising chicks. Hares should be hopping through the thickets, ears tuned for danger. I stroll along, thinking about the forest and all its communities. It's always seemed strange to me that humans are so curious about life on other planets and know so little about the other worlds that share the Earth.

That evening I eat cheese and nuts while I walk. More and more spruce islands appear. The trail is muddy and rutted with moose and caribou tracks. No tracks that look like a barefoot human's; no bears.

And then the clumps of brush become a forest. The trail is boggy and a gray thrush is trilling from a treetop. "You should fly away," I call in his direction. "Can't you feel the frost?"

I find a flat area where the river bends and make camp on a bed of moss. All night a chinook blasts heat like a furnace over the mountain peaks.

In the morning the tent is steaming hot. I slide out through the front, shedding my bag inside. There's an endless supply of dead branches to snap off for my fire. I carve a spoon from a chunk of cottonwood bark while I wait for my pot to boil. The forest is noisy with gray jays and tiny black-capped chickadees and rustling leaves.

On the spine of a hill, caribou mill about, digging for lichen, all skinny legs and antlers in the distance.

I am happy, relaxed at last.

The trouble is that I'm growing up. Becky has known what she wanted since she was small. She loves to run dogs and her life just falls into place around it. Maybe I should have taken an extra year to finish school, not a year less. Becky has to stay in shape. She has to work at two jobs in the summer to support her team and run them every day in the winter. Most winters there's a litter of pups, and she sells all but the smartest and fastest. She goes where she likes, wandering miles and miles of trails with her dogs. Mom only asks that she draw a route map on a white board before she leaves. But how do I make a life from fairy tales and juggling, and the memory of a clearing in a forest long ago and far away, and a father who was either a kindly king or a humble woodcutter, depending on how you look at it?

"For heaven's sake, Rachel," said Mom, brushing my hair from my forehead. "None of the endings are actually true. They're just stories. Somebody made them up. It doesn't matter if it's the author's ending or mine or yours."

This was serious. Didn't Mom know that I dreamed of a lake? The water was blue and cliffs rose from it, and white birds roosted on the rocks and wheeled over its surface. And all true stories flowed from that lake, that beautiful lake. Endings couldn't be changed simply because somebody wanted happiness. For heaven's sake, dragons and prison guards patrolled its entrance. Princesses and princes had died, falling gallantly from overhanging boulders, yearning to reach the water nestled below them.

After many days of wandering through the wild forest, the princess wheeled her steed about and drew up beside the prince's. "We could die here," she said. "I'm afraid."

The prince nodded his head and reached across to touch her hand.

Side by side, they trotted up a grassy slope until the horses could climb no more. Then the princess and the prince dismounted and set forth by foot through the enchanted forest, their hands on the sheaths of their swords, for there were many dangers...

Of course, I didn't say all that, or even think it clearly, when I was small. But I kind of did. Fairy tales were sacred to me, nothing to be messed with. But because I couldn't put it into words, I only kissed Mom and let her snuff out the light with her breath, quiet and warm in the darkness.

I've changed since the bear came into camp. Grizzly and polar bears can breed—pizzlies, they're called, or grolar bears. They're so new that there isn't an established word yet. Maybe polar bears are wandering farther inland from the melting ice these days and meeting up with grizzlies they once evolved from. A grizzly and black bear supposedly mated in a London zoo, but their offspring didn't live. Is the golden bear a hybrid who has somehow managed to grow up? And be beautiful.

Grizzlies are considered to be a symbol of wilderness because they need such an enormous range to thrive. Without an intact ecosystem to roam through, grizzlies die off. It's not enough to preserve bits of habitat here and there: grizzlies need to wander.

I tie a pouch at my belt and drop my bear spray and banger into it for easy reach. Whenever I see spots moving in the trees, my hand cups the top of the pouch and gently tugs it free, like a cowboy drawing his six-shooter.

It's different traveling in the forest. I miss the open land and the smell of Labrador tea when I lie on my stomach and willow smoke when I blow twigs into flame. The woods are to my left, dropping to the river. Beyond the forest on my right rise mountains: the lower slopes are dark with buckbrush; the upper slopes are bright with glistening outcrops of rock.

Every day I'm remembering more about Dad. Sometimes I can open the door to the past and he's waiting inside. One memory will spark so many others, like a line of fire-crackers when the fuse is lit. When that happens, it doesn't feel like I'm remembering. It's like I'm actually there.

The funny thing is that I'm different in those memories. I'm not a very emotional person. It's only when I'm in the room of memories with Dad that I'm light and happy. I feel free. Until I remember—quickly as a curtain shutting off the stage—he's gone.

I see the bear in the heat of the afternoon, a yellow swath over a dark shape lumbering far off through the trees. He's gone so fast, I'm not sure it's really him. Brooks growls and stiffens by my side.

I camp where I turn off from the forest to climb another pass. Although I've already eaten a cold supper while I walked, I light a fire and lie stretched beside it while the bowl of stars and the northern lights shimmer across the darkness.

From now until almost at the cabin, there is no more trail. If I don't read the map properly, I'll get lost. I'll turn around and the mountains will all look the same no matter which direction I turn.

"Follow a creek," Mom said. "All the creeks flow north into the same river. When you get to the river, walk to the cabin if you know which direction it's in. If you don't, stay visible on the bank and we'll find you. Don't go back into the forest. Don't leave the water. Make a decent camp and relax. We'll come eventually."

For days she'd been giving me so much advice that I couldn't take it all in. She'd mentioned this already at least three times.

"Mom," I sighed, my hand on her shoulder, "I'll be just fine."

7

Panic

In the morning, fear is dancing like dust motes in the air. I can't keep still. A cooling wind blows through my head, freezing my thoughts. A natural theater of jagged mountains is to the right of my camp. I poke at last night's fire with a stick, and a cloud of ash billows up, making me cough. I heap lichen on still-red coals and blow until they flame a pale yellow.

Then I pace.

Snow streams out from the peaks I'm heading toward, like schools of fish darting through currents of air. If I broke camp and walked, I could get to the cabin without sleeping properly again. I could just head directly there, nap and walk, nap and walk. Dad's handiwork will be all over the clearing and in the cabin and down the trails we made when we lived there. Dad's blazes will be on the spruce trees, showing the way, marks from his ax fading into the tree trunks.

Mom told me she put our gear in the cache, as well as leftover food. Did she put in everything? Will his coffee cup be sitting on the counter? Will his frying pan be hanging on a nail above the stove and will his ax be stuck in the chopping block? Mom was looking for clues, not aiming for a clean camp.

Panic sweeps over me. My breath comes in quick ragged gasps.

He wanted to come back. He told me he would.

He could be anywhere, of course. Maybe he never came back to the cabin. Maybe the memories hurt him too much, so he just wanders about from camp to camp through the mountains, always on the move. Maybe he's okay as long as he doesn't have to damp down the restlessness churning inside him.

I stoop and stroke Brooks's back. I'm still growing. At this rate I'll soon have to kneel to pat him. What with walking all day and growing, I'm probably starving myself. Maybe I wouldn't panic so fast if I just had more food.

I stand, feet slightly apart, elbows at my sides, and swivel my body, each time bringing it back to home position. After a few minutes, I pick up my juggling balls and warm up. I toss one ball behind my back and up and retrieve it with the other hand. Smooth and relaxed. Smooth and relaxed. Over and up into the other hand, with always an instant where the audience can no longer see the ball. From now on, there's no more trail. I'll just follow the river.

When we're dreaming—or remembering—time doesn't exist.

The balls cascade out from the center, and I remember Dad in the sunshine on the gravel bar with his baseball cap on and his fishing rod flying out from his shoulder. I stacked rocks for a castle by his side. A warm breeze blew from the passes where the creek flowed down from the mountains. When I was little, I was sure I heard beautiful music, barely audible, on the wind. Mom and Becky were somewhere close by, and when I turned from my make-believe world to fill my pot with river water for a moat, I saw smoke rising from our chimney and drifting to fill the wild forest around our hut.

Dad smelled like wood smoke and tobacco. So did the air about me. Peace buzzed through the air and landed lightly on us and made me smile. Did we live happily ever after?

I didn't know what happiness was then, but I lived in it; I breathed it in.

I finish juggling with a high throw. While the third ball is overhead, I clap my right hand to my left, transferring its ball. I catch the high ball with my empty hand, letting only my arms do the work.

Brooks sits before me, eyes tracing each movement.

"Let's take the day off, Brooks," I say, packing the balls away for the day.

An idea comes to me as I speak. "We'll just leave everything here and walk up this draw along the creek. Maybe I'll see something with the monocle from the ridge."

I fill Brooks's pack with cheese and nuts, drop the monocle in a shirt pocket and snap on my waist belt filled with bangers and bear spray and bug dope. We climb a knoll through dwarf birch and look back at my camp. A smudge of campfire smoke still drifts across the tundra. I think about returning to put it out, but the tundra is wet. It shouldn't burn.

The brush is thick, and I need both arms to push my way through. Brooks gets stuck again and again with his pack. He whines and turns to bite himself free. I haul on his collar.

I haven't eaten breakfast. I put my hands on my stomach. It's sunken in. I'm not hungry, of course. At home I mostly eat in bed at night while I read. Here I can't do that.

Ahead I see an open patch covered with dried bear-berry and blueberry leaves like a splash of spilled red wine. The golden bear is grazing in the berry patch. He is minding his own business, shoveling berries—leaves and all—between his loose black lips. Startled, he glances over at us and shakes his head.

Brooks dashes to the bear and stands by its head, barking his foolish head off. Like a boxer, he dances back and forth.

The bear lifts his massive head, crowberry plants trailing out both sides of his mouth.

Brooks nips at its front leg. Like a demented terrier, he grasps the leg between his jaws, his whole body tossing with the effort.

"Brooks!"

No response.

The bear makes a grating sound like he's grinding his teeth.

"Come!"

I see a paw with claws like hunting knives reach up and swipe through the bright air. Then Brooks is on the ground, lost under a mountain of shaking fur.

"No!" Not my voice. Not my voice at all.

Brooks screams; the bear grunts. Brooks is between the bear's jaws now, being shaken back and forth like a towel. His ears hang down.

I screw the cylinder of gunpowder into the banger.

I want to run. It's such an enormous effort not to.

Instead I point the banger into the air and then lower it a fraction so the flare will explode slightly toward me. I don't want the bear to be scared in my direction. I pull back on the safety and, almost in the same motion, grab my bear spray from its holster and yank off its safety just in case the bear won't leave.

The flare explodes with an orange tail.

The bear is running low to the ground. I see his yellow stripe rippling from head to tail, shoulder hump pumping as he escapes. Pee dribbles between his back legs. I can smell it, sour and hot.

I screw in another flare and watch it explode.

Willow branches snap back and forth. Behind the bear, bushes shake until gradually they still.

No birds.

Brooks lies on the ground without moving, his green pack ripped open.

The cheese is bloody. So are the nuts. Brooks's blood blends with the red plants of the tundra.

I pick up the empty gunpowder shells from the earth and stick them in my pocket. I don't know why; they're completely useless but I want to hang on to them.

Then someone is screaming. Noises pour from my mouth. I fold my arms around my chest to keep them in.

Everything I love disappears. I'll never see our cabin again. My father won't come back. And now, neither will Brooks. There's just loss, like the ball at hip level vanishing behind my back with a slight upward tilt.

"Becky's happy," said Mom. "She runs her dogs and she's living her own dreams. You need to let go of what happened to Dad. Remember the good times and what he was like then."

"But there's nothing left, Mom," I said.

"You'll always have your memories."

"You can't eat memories," I said, before I could think. "And nothing else tastes good."

I put my arms around Brooks's neck and hold him. I'm lying on blood. I wriggle out of my sweater and place it on his flank, behind his pack.

My feelings are still somewhat frozen, but my memories are growing stronger. They unfold with all my senses involved: sight and smell and hearing and touch and even taste. They're a time machine, and I can work the controls at will. It's just a little trickier staying in the present.

Then Brooks picks up his head and licks my face.

He's alive.

Barely, but he's alive.

If he has to die, I want him to die this very second. That way neither of us will suffer. It's childish and it's selfish and I shouldn't feel like that. But for this moment, I do.

I take the bags of bloody cheese and nuts and hurl them with all my strength down the mountain. Then I stand, hands over my face, and force myself to breathe slowly. It's so hard to tear away my hands. I don't want to see mountains all around me. I don't want to see that I'm completely alone.

The pack saved his life. The fabric is torn and the deepest wound slashes along his left flank, sparing his belly. The rest are just scratches.

"It's okay, puppy," I murmur. "It's okay." I don't look too closely or I'll throw up.

I knot the pack around my waist and spend a few minutes searching with the monocle for an open route down the draw back to camp. Brooks lies on his belly and licks his wound. For a moment I scan farther. No smoke, no hidden camps with Dad about to charge out and help.

I scoop Brooks into my arms so he lies crosswise with his wound on the outside. Good thing I'm used to carrying a heavy pack. I carry Brooks as far as I can down the mountain.

When I collapse, I stroke him, both of us lying on the slope.

Without warning, I'm mad. Anger breaks over me. "What an idiot! The bear just wanted to be left alone. Was that too much to ask?"

I stand and walk off a few steps.

Brooks drags himself behind me.

"You could have got me killed too," I shout.

Brooks lies perfectly still on his belly and whines.

My stomach cramps. I retch into the willows but nothing comes out. I haven't eaten since yesterday. The ravens can devour the bloody lunch for all I care. Silence screeches in my ears. What am I doing? Brooks is in pain. And there's no one else here to take charge.

"Come on, Brooks," I coax.

Sunshine disappears from the valley below. Stars wink overhead.

"You can do it, puppy," I tell him.

And he does, dragging one leg.

We get back to camp in the dark. I grope in my pack for my flashlight. I poke in the fire-pit ashes for a spark, but nothing glows. I'm trembling with cold and shock. It's too dark to find kindling. I need to calm down, to focus on something else. That's what my story does, I think. It takes me somewhere else.

The prince and the princess were still on their quest, searching for the lake of true stories where the white birds roosted, when the prince was captured by the Guardians of the Lake. Days of wandering later, the princess too was discovered. She was sleeping in a sun-drenched glade, sparrows twittering on branches above her grass bed, bees lazily droning amongst yellow poppies and blue gentians.

The guards led the princess to the stone-walled dungeon. One guard marched ahead, holding an oil lamp. The princess ran her hand along the wall as she stumbled through the dark hallways, hoping to memorize the return route. They slammed the cell door. She watched the last flicker of light retreat. The dungeon smelled of mold. Far off she heard water dripping.

I haul Brooks to the tent door and push him in.

He smells like meat and fresh blood. The smell will advertise us to animals passing in the night. Don't think about it, I tell myself. Lock the image of that bear out of your mind.

I sit down, kick off my boots, arrange my defenses inside one boot by my head and go to sleep, an arm flung over Brooks. I will myself not to dream. In the morning, I think, I'll decide what to do. It wasn't the bear's fault. It's not like he was vicious or cruel. He was only trying to eat some berries.

My sleep is empty, a long blank hallway with slammed doors on both sides. When I wake once, I force myself to concentrate on my story.

In the Dungeon

Then began a dark time for the princess. There was no action possible. Nothing changed or happened for such a long time that she was unaware of the passage of time. But still, in the distance, water dripped. Soon she realized someone was whistling in time to the drops.

"Who is it?" called the princess, standing to attention in the blackness. She was so relieved to hear her voice, any voice, that she shouted it again and again.

"No need to shout," said a cheerful voice in return. "Talk softly and I'll walk to your voice."

It was the prince, her beloved prince. She was no longer alone.

✷

"Oh, Brooks," I choke out. He whines and licks his wound. I play with his droopy ears and then slide out. Blackflies are waiting on the screen. They swarm my face, crawling into the creases by my eyes and behind my ears. I smear their carcasses into my sweat. Brooks has to get better, because I sure don't know what to do.

✷

In the darkness, touch is the loudest sense.

The prince dropped to his knees before the princess and kissed her clammy hand until it prickled with warmth.

✷

Brooks is licking my hand, serious washing licks.

"Cut it out!"

The sun is already high. It's another hot fall day in the forest. I light a fire, and when the twigs and branches have caught, I coax Brooks to join me. He lies by the fire on his belly. I boil water and drink hot juice from powder. I boil water again and add oats and butter and dried fruit. Brooks's wound gapes open. I see the skin layer and under-neath it—steak. How does something with a personality become meat? His ears are soft as Arctic cotton grass. When I stroke them, he slides closer to me so his head rests on my lap. He thinks I can make him better, I guess.

I eat slowly with my cottonwood spoon, forcing myself to swallow. Halfway through the pot, the porridge begins to taste good: hot and sweet. I finish it fast before my stomach rebels and then shove the pot to Brooks to lick.

He doesn't even turn his head. Seems the last of his energy went into cleaning my hand.

It's farther back to the road than if we go on to the cabin. At the cabin Brooks can snooze in comfort by the woodstove. So should I stay put or continue? It's only growing colder.

At the cabin I can heat water in the washbasin and thoroughly clean his wound. There should be old dog food and, most important, there should be salt in the cache for soaking the cut. I have a couple of spoonfuls that will have to do until we get there. Mom always uses salt for keeping cuts from getting infected.

And, of course, if I go back now I'll never know what happened to Dad.

But will Brooks make it?

Gray jays light on the spruce branches hanging far above the flames. Downriver, a raven caws and slowly flaps toward us. White dots slide over the mountain. When I focus the monocle, I see ewes and lambs napping in the afternoon heat on a rocky shelf, fresh snow patches directly above them.

I wash the pot in the creek and dip its bottom lip under the green water to fill. I hang a pole over the fire, weighing the end with stones so it hangs at the right angle. When the water's hot, I pour some in my cup with a pinch of salt, find a clean (more or less) sock and pour the lukewarm water over Brooks's cut. He yowls and snaps at my hand. Instantly sorry, he nuzzles into my leg.

"Don't worry, pup," I say, stroking his head.

While he sleeps, I toss my sleeping bag over some branches to air, and I open the tent windows to let breezes play through the screen.

Restlessness burns through my muscles. My thighs twitch.

I can see the cabin clearly in my mind. I see myself with Brooks, walking down the last miles of foot trail and then cutting across the clearing. I feel myself pulling back on the hammer so its head eases out the spikes that hold the window shutters in place.

What I don't see is what the cabin looks like inside now I'm grown up. I've never been there alone without everyone else's gear cluttering the space.

Brooks can sleep by the woodstove until he's better. I can leave him safely inside while I look for clues to Dad's disappearance. At night I'll go to bed within four log walls that hold years of memories, the fire banked and smoldering in the stove. Red coals, flames yellow and blue.

What if the bear comes back? What if he won't leave us alone?

That's ridiculous to even imagine. The bear must have way better things to do with his time than follow us.

After a supper of cheese and crackers, I can no longer force myself to sit still. I break camp. I've made my decision. If I don't get there this time, I'll probably never try again.

I stuff the gear from Brooks's torn pack into mine. I'll sew it at the cabin. Now I'm in shape, I don't notice the extra weight. I shrug the pack over my shoulders.

I douse the flames completely. The charred bones of branches collapse on the downy ashes. Brooks lies with his eyes closed, curled in a ball, his wound on the outside flank.

"Let's go, boy."

Brooks stares at me, astounded, and pushes his muzzle into my ankle.

I kneel down, my pack almost toppling me. I haul him up by his collar. "Sorry, Brooks. Staying put's not an option. We need salt and food."

Brooks takes a step using three legs, then sits, eyes locked with mine.

I snap the leash to his collar and tug. "Come on, pup."

And that's how we walk out of the forest and into the high country again. We rest every few minutes. I stand, leaning forward to take the weight off my shoulders. Brooks crashes on his rear and slurps at his cut.

Sometimes I shout to warn the bear we are coming. Sometimes I keep very still. I will be so happy if Brooks recovers. Funny, though, because yesterday he was healthy, and I wasn't happy then.

I don't know how best to avoid this bear. He needs lots of notice before we show up again to bug him. In the end, I yodel maybe once every five minutes. In between yodels I try to imagine my way back into the story of the princess's quest, but I can't concentrate.

When the last light is blazing from the mountain faces about me, I pitch my tent on a small knoll where I can see the valley spread below. The brush grows in patches lower than my waist. Far away, the river gleams silver. Under my tent is a bed of soft deep moss. I hold Brooks curled into my side all night and fall into a restless sleep. There's something about moss I should remember.

Asleep, my dreams are confusing and not about the quest at all. I dream that my father is in a hut at the edge of a forest, ax in hand. He stares down the path at the thud of approaching hooves. A nightingale sings in a cottonwood by the bank.

I dig in my heels and gallop toward him. "Dad!"

My father's face is yearning, his arms outstretched.

Then he covers his face with his hands.

When he removes them, fur is growing on his cheeks. He snarls, showing yellow teeth, and holds his hands in front of his face, staring at them. Claws curl crooked at their ends, shining like knives.

I jerk back on the reins.

The tent and knoll are bathed in moonlight. Wind surges from the passes like a faraway tide. It was just a nightmare. The bear, I'm sure, is nowhere around.

✳

*"What do you love doing?" asked Mom, whittling a chunk of
poplar bark into the shape of a wolf. She dug the knife in hard
and blew away splinters of wood from a leg.*

*I leaned against a tree trunk in the sunshine and opened
my eyes, content to be with her.*

"Lots of things," I said.

*Mom held her carving up to show me. "What are you doing
when you're the happiest?"*

*I love mountains and forests and fairy tales and juggling
and being alone, I think. And I love you too, Mom.*

✳

Pain rattles like stones in my stomach. Mouth dry, I listen
to Brooks's ragged breath. Moonlight is so strange in
the mountains. Every detail is transformed, washed in
soft underwater light. I watch through the screen door.
I think of my father's face in my dream, before it changed,
before he snarled and his warm hands grew to claws.
Shrugging off the dream, I roll over but my fingers graze
Brooks's side. I draw them back into my sleeping bag,
sticky with blood.

Later, I crouch over Brooks, who doesn't want to move
from the morning fire. "Come on, boy," I coax. "You have
to eat."

I shove the porridge pot under his nose. "Sit," I say, firmly.

Joanne Bell

What I mean is "stand" but he doesn't know the command for that.

His head stays flat on the ground. Only his tail thumps feebly on the moss.

I dip my finger into the porridge and shove it in his mouth. Brooks swallows and lumbers to three of his feet. The fourth is tucked up under the wounded flank. He takes forever to lick the pot clean. By the time I've loaded my pack and washed his wound, the sun is splashing the mountains with shafts of shadow and light.

We walk maybe a mile that day, through high country, above the tree line. Brooks hops on three legs the entire way. I make camp at the top of the second pass, with only a few willow twigs for fuel. Soon it won't matter that I need to force myself to eat. At this rate, we'll be almost out of food by the time we reach the cabin. We've eaten the last of the dry meat and bananas and cheese. There are still plenty of dried vegetables for broth, but that won't give us much energy.

Before stopping for a cold supper the next day, I see bear tracks on the sandy bank of a creek crossing. All bear tracks look like they were made by a huge barefoot human. Grizzly claws, however, are longer than blacks', and the curve of the toes is flatter. A little farther along I see scat, stuffed with berries and purplish leaves. I growl at the mess and boot it apart with a branch. I sniff hard. Nothing. Just the faraway smell of winter coming, of snow dusting the peaks. It can't be the same bear. Male grizzlies have an enormous range, but why would he still be heading in our direction? It must be another bear just passing through.

I snatch gloves from my pack pocket and pull them on.

We've walked almost across the pass now. But where the mountains draw back a bit, a narrow creek tumbles into the valley, flowing into what's now a river. Clumps of cottonwood and alder grow along it. I walk through the trunks in the late afternoon with sunshine slanting along the ground. A few spruce grow among them.

I see the blaze at twilight. It's definitely not the scratch lines of a bear or the gnawing of a porcupine. I run my fingers over the marks of the ax on the trunk. How many years has it been there? I walk by instinct, following the faint opening through the trees. If I concentrate too hard, I'll lose the way. Eventually I stumble on another blaze, and another, both on young black spruce trees.

Then a stump, cut by a swede saw. The wood has yellowed over its scar. There are several stumps, and I can just make out an unbroken horizontal line. Little in nature is so straight. Logs are stacked on each other for walls. From the sod roof, grass and a few fingers of willow reach tentatively for the darkening sky.

Thank god, I think. A safe place to spend the night: a cottage in the forest.

9

Moving On

Clumps of willows hide the closed door. Raspberry and rosehip bushes tangle against the log walls. Empty windows trail strips of moldering cloth like prayer flags. I unbolt the door and push hard. It doesn't budge.

It's not our main cabin, of course—just some little line cabin that someone once threw up for overnights while traveling. I must have been here when I was little, but I can't remember, though it seems familiar. The building has sunk crookedly into the permafrost, taking the doorframe with it. No way will it open without the floor inside being dug out.

I crawl in through the window hole and squint into the gloom.

An ax lies flat on a drying rack above a tin cookstove.

"Yes!" I shout to Brooks, who's waiting outside. I chop at the floorboards until I can swing the door open. Brooks slinks in and collapses, exhausted. Shafts of evening light stream through, revealing a filthy floor littered with squirrel debris: cones, dried mushrooms, tattered cloth.

A white quarter moon floats into a V between peaks and hangs in the branches of a cottonwood. A twig broom stands behind the door. I sweep the floor and the pole bed at the far wall by flashlight. In my pack is a box of candles. I place one on a table and one in an iron candleholder jutting out from between two logs. A box of kindling and another of spruce chunks is by the stove. It's all familiar, I realize, lighting the fire. I've been here before—I must have been really little.

I wait outside while the chimney clears; then I make the bed, keeping the door open, working by the moonlight slanting over the floorboards. Pictures are tacked along the walls, cutouts from magazines. In the dusk I can't make out what they are. I tuck my tent into one window hole and my tarp into the other to keep in the warmth.

I pry the lid from a tin: smells like black tea. I boil water in my own pot and throw in a pinch of the leaves. Maybe Dad stayed here. Maybe he lived here for a long time while Mom searched the cabin and we stayed with the neighbors. Maybe he was returning to us, and he found this place and hurt himself somehow. In the morning I'll look for a note. If he had no paper, a message could be carved into a log on the wall.

Brooks has managed to hop to the stove's side, where he moans and nips at his wound frantically. I get out my spare shirt and dribble it with warm water and my last spoonful of salt. It's easier when I can't see the marbled steak of his flank.

Grunting, I heave Brooks onto the bed and lie down, cocooned by the sturdy walls and the glow of flames through the stove's open draft. Logs settle as they burn, and a breeze plays in the willows snug against the cabin. I wake once when a wind shoots suddenly from the peaks, rattling the stovepipe, plucking at the river's surface and slamming on through the night. Then the rhythmic wind and the water lull me back to sleep.

I was very small, and everything was extremely interesting to me. A pack of wolves had been playing near the little line cabin, two days' short walk from our main cabin. Every morning and afternoon and evening they howled from all directions, but mostly from the hill where Becky and I tobogganed.

"That's it. I'm leaving."

"Where are you going?" Dad was stirring a five-gallon tin bucket full of dog scraps and grain. It was suspended from a tripod over a bonfire in the clearing. He held the wooden paddle flat in front of him and twirled it once, then twice, like a baton. Then he bowed.

"I'm getting one, Dad," I told him, pulling my snow pants over my boots. "I'm getting a baby wolf."

Dad followed me down the trail, which was soft and soggy in the spring sunshine. The wolves had a den nearby. Dad's weight made him sink while I barely scratched the snow's surface.

"Go home," I said. "Wolves don't like grown-ups."

"Nah," said Dad, shaking snow on us both from an overhanging spruce bough. "But they probably like their pups. They'd be sad if you took one home."

"They'd still have some left," I reminded him.

"We'd have Becky if you ran away. But it wouldn't make us not sad."

I leaped at his legs, signaling forgiveness. "Don't worry," I reassured him when he squatted down so I could hop on for a piggyback. "I won't run away yet."

One moment I'm sleeping, the next listening, fully alert.

Wolves are calling from beyond the river. They sing to each other like chanting monks and break off one at a time. I disentangle myself from Brooks and sit up in the dark.

A lone wolf cries from the other side of the cabin. Brooks is lying on my bag, growling deep in his throat.

I swing off the bed and crack the door. Cold blasts in; I rub my bare feet against each other. Moments ago I was safely asleep.

Becky said that each wolf in a pack howls at a different pitch to make it sound as if there are more than there really are. She also said that wolves can hear at a much higher range than humans and stake their territory for absent members of the pack by scent marking as well as howling.

Eyes shining, a pack of wolves stands in the moonlit forest, spread out in a straight line. They're so close I can see their fur is wet from wading across to me. Only my head sticks from behind the door. They pace forward, holding my stare, tails level with their spines.

I open my mouth to yell "GET!" but it comes out soft, like a breath.

They splash away across the river and mill about on the far bank like they're waiting for a signal to proceed. A few sit on their haunches like dogs. One stretches his front legs and yawns.

"Now you can get," I call across. From behind me comes the howl of the lone wolf. The northern lights are a smudge of green dancing above the horizon. The sky is enormous.

I'm surrounded.

"Enough," I shout, mustering a firm voice. "Wolves don't attack people. GET OUT OF HERE!"

Anything can happen in here. Dad could stroll up the bank or I could hear shots popping in time to the northern lights and follow them tomorrow to a dugout with Dad's stovepipe jutting from a bank. The tide of his disappearance will wash away from my life, and nothing will be smashed where it's flowed.

Heads slightly lowered, the wolves twist around and slide back into the willows, outlines broken by branches moving as they retreat.

Slowly, the twigs stop trembling and shine, motionless once more in the moonlight. My heart is banging against my chest.

I slam the door and climb into bed. Brooks washes my face and I shove him away and listen for the lone wolf, the lookout, arm slung for comfort over Brooks's chest.

The sun's already high across the mountains beyond the far bank when I wake next. In that first moment before I can really remember where I am, before my eyes slip open and meet Brooks's, I'm happy. I slip on my boots and blow the fire's coals into life.

Brooks dangles his head over the edge of the pole bed and barks. "No problem," I say. "You just had to ask."

I lift him down and he walks, stiff-legged, out the open door. He puts his paw on the ground but with no weight on it.

Outside, there's no sign of any life. I grin and duck back in: four walls, unpeeled roof poles, stove, table and two shelves, all made from poles. The wolf pack that surrounded me feels like a dream in the hot sunshine. An enamel cup and a frying pan hang above the table. Magazine cutouts of beautiful women in one-piece bathing suits line the walls;

their hair is curled and tucked neatly behind their ears. The shelf beside the stove holds several tins: tea, flour and a bitter white powder I guess is baking powder.

I lift each picture off its nail and check the underside for notes. Those pictures were there all my life; some long-ago trapper who built the cabin tacked them into place and we left them up. Becky and I thought they were beautiful mothers because their breasts were so huge.

There's no sign of Dad.

Outside, the river curves merrily around bends, forest lining its banks. On the rises above, caribou move single file up a draw. I mix the flour and baking powder with fresh water and fry the cake in butter on the stove. Brooks stretches by the heat. No salt. I've used the small amount I carried to bathe his cut.

In a moment my mood shifts.

There is no salt left. Brooks's wound is sealing shut. I can only hope there's no infection, no poison inside. I juggle while the bannock fries, trying to forget the emptiness here: a regular and then a reverse cascade, then a new trick running the balls behind one knee.

The bannock smells delicious. I break off a crunchy bit and pop it in my mouth, dunked in the spluttering butter.

It tastes moldy.

I spit on the ground outside. Maybe the tea last night was moldy too, and I was too tired to tell. Maybe I'll be throwing up for days. I clutch my stomach, but it just feels hollowed out, as usual.

I can't hear any approaching animal with the river so close. I poke around outside for a while, searching for a cache. Maybe there's some food that hasn't absorbed any moisture.

A raven drops suddenly from a cottonwood and circles the cabin. Dad and I used to talk to ravens, but I've never noticed them properly since he left: enormous, black, shiny ventriloquists. He loved ravens, and wherever he stayed, a few would eventually land, knowing he was good for some leftovers.

I throw the remaining bannock under the tree for the raven. He lands on a branch and makes pinging noises like a knuckle rapping a crystal glass.

Brooks dutifully barks.

Ravens hang out in Becky's dog yard every day. They land just out of reach of the chained huskies and strut around while the dogs yowl and strain. When the dogs finally back away from the end of their chains, the ravens hop in and scoop up any leftover tidbits of frozen dog food they can find. Wild ravens live about twenty-five years. Parrots of the North, Becky calls them. A pair of them lived for decades in the Tower of London, able to talk because their tongues had been split.

"Big price for the ravens," I remember Dad saying.

The raven hops down from his perch and toddles toward us, feathers puffed.

How many years would a raven remember?

Could this bird be so friendly because he's been around Dad lately?

He snatches the bannock from the ground where I've tossed it and tears off a corner.

I hope it doesn't make him sick.

"Where's my father?" I whisper. Ravens are magnificent. This one is halfway up to my knees. If they weren't so common, people would be awed by them. I've seen them scare off eagles that were lunching from a salmon on a gravel bar near town. The ravens yanked at the eagles' tail feathers.

Wind funnels through the valley all day, smelling of snow. I spread the contents of my pack in front of the south wall in the sunshine, blocked from the gusts. I count how many meals I have left. There's no butter, cheese, chocolate or nuts, only dry food. Not enough to get us to the cabin. I sure haven't eaten much, but I've chucked a lot to Brooks. He'll have to limp faster and farther when really he should rest.

I think about staying in the line cabin until Brooks has healed up.

But I can't.

There's not enough food. And Mom wouldn't know where I was. There'd be a search party out for me this time. I can't do that to her.

Somehow the silence seems stronger where there was once someone living. All my life I've wanted to come back to our cabin. The wind blows and blows, and I can't feel any warmth from the sun even in the shelter of the old cabin.

I've never thought beyond searching for Dad. I've never considered what my life will be like when I know what happened to him. What will I make of my life? It's always been one howl of panic echoing through the years: He said he'd return. Every morning since he left, I've woken, probing my memory like an abscessed tooth until I get busy just to distract myself from the pain.

Brooks snatches, growling, at his flank. His wound is still festering. Wolves must die of such infections all the time.

"Daddy," I whisper, just to hear a voice. "I learned how to juggle."

The sick part is that I can hear him answer after all these years. His breath brushes against my ears. His grin grows crooked before my eyes.

"What for?" asks my dad.

I stumble into my pack and start out again while the sun slides down toward another mountaintop. There's no trail anymore; we've walked beyond it. Sometimes I follow game trails along the river. Always, they end in a tangle of fallen brush. At least there'll be leftover food at our old cabin, and salt to soak Brooks's cut. At least there'll be a warm, clean spot for him to sleep beside the stove.

I watch for blazes on the trees. There are always trees now. The tundra is windswept and beautiful and vast behind us. The gusts have blown from the north. Snow clouds sail across the sky.

I'm on my way again, Brooks limping by my side.

10

In the Forest

As we descend through the forest, the walking becomes slower as the undergrowth thickens, and at times white spruce trees laden with boughs lie crashed across our path. Brooks can plod for a few hours at a time but I always need to lift him over obstacles. When I hold him in my arms against my chest, I feel a surge of tenderness.

I see no bear scat or tracks, but once I notice a rotting log that has been clawed apart by something massive. I can't tell how long ago it happened. Brooks's wound crusts and is torn open by a jutting branch so that blood bubbles and beads along its length.

In the late afternoon I stretch out on some moss and sleep, my pack as my pillow. Brooks curls up, sheltered in the crook of my arm. When I wake, there is fresh blood like berry stains on the earth. I turn him gently in the slanting sunshine and notice pus seething beneath the surface.

"You need to lie still, Brooks. And get more salt water on that cut."

Brooks whimpers. Holding his nose in one hand, I kiss it.

The cabin is only a few miles away. I stir juice crystals into hot water and sip a while, trying to calm myself. I give Brooks most of my watery porridge and set out.

Brooks moves like a marionette jerked slowly by its strings. He still doesn't put any weight on the leg beneath his wound.

"We're not stopping until we're home." He needs to lie still until he's healed. Brooks whines, pausing every few minutes to snatch with his mouth at his wound as we walk. I listen for the sound of branches cracking above the surge of water as I continue the tale.

The princess freed herself from the dungeon but lost the prince in the confusion of the escape. In the light of day, she noticed a smear of blood across her shoulder where the prince had brushed against her. Unable to find him, she searched for the dragon whose cave blocked the entrance to the lake from which all true stories flow. She found the dragon's prints followed by a trough where his tail had dragged behind. The prince's footprints were almost obscured by those of the dragon. It was hard

to track either one clearly because the ground where the dragon had passed was bare and scorched.

And so the princess set out to slay the dragon. Fearful that the prince would not survive, she led her exhausted horse deeper and deeper into the heart of the forest. In a tangled thicket, the dragon lurked in a cave that burrowed far beneath the earth. Along its corridors the dragon had hoarded not only its treasures, but also the bones of those who had come upon the dragon's lair.

The moon had risen and the forest was bathed in its blue glow. Still the princess jumped at every cracking branch, and no birds sang.

I snap Brooks onto his leash so he keeps up with me and continue hunting for a game trail in the tangled willows along the bank. From beside me, I hear the jerky rhythm of his gait.

After many days the princess stood with her horse beside a stream that gurgled through the moss. A black enchanted bird wheeled above her, claws extended, wings silken smooth with serrated tips. He dropped down and perched beside her, barely missing her head.

"What are you searching for?" croaked the bird, snatching a round blackberry from the moss, then another.

"The dragon," said the princess, looking up from her reflection in the water. "I cannot return until I've slain the dragon."

"Then you won't return," said the bird, "until all happiness has shriveled away."

He hopped a few steps and viciously pecked at a berry the princess held cupped in the palm of her hand. Sticky black juice pooled on her palm.

"And what," he said, "would be the point of that?"

"But I'm not happy now," said the princess.

"Taste it," ordered the raven pushing her fingers with his beak. The berry was sour, and the princess spat it out.

Then she quietly turned away, paying no more heed to the enchanted bird. But as she traveled on, her worthy steed lagged farther and farther behind until one day his legs crumpled beneath him and he lay on the forest floor. Grave with disappointment, his eyes searched hers until they closed.

The princess wept silently, but still she carried on.

The only trail I find is a low tunnel I have to stoop through. A black pat of bear scat lies directly before me.

"Idiot," I tell myself, out loud. Meat-eating bears have black smelly scat filled with hair and bone. I do a breast-stroke-like motion through the thick brush, yodeling constantly, until I'm back in the spruce trees.

Eyes burning, the princess wandered on through the tangled forest so slowly that the fallen trees she'd clambered over in the morning were still visible in the moonlight.

Again the enchanted bird lit on a branch beside her.

"Princess," said the bird, "you must return, for you are in great danger."

"What danger?" snapped the princess. "It seems I'm not the one who has paid the price."

"Only this," said the raven. "That your life is going by without you."

"Are you looking for me?" The gruff voice of the dragon drifted through the night air.

He slid belly-first into the stream, like a shark breaking the smooth surface of the waters with his fiery snout.

The raven rose and tumbled, then rose again, flying frantically until lost from sight.

Up and up the bank, the dragon scrambled toward the princess. Dripping water, he breathed hot stale steam on her innocent face.

But in that moment, something happened. Time in all of its grace stopped, and she was no longer afraid.

A quiet happiness seemed to blow through the clearing and the still air, filling her senses with every shallow shaking breath she breathed. The princess stood very still and listened and waited.

The world about her grew brighter and clearer, and on the horizon a completely different bird—a hawk of mottled plumage—hung in the vortex of a warm current of air, riding its draft to the heavens. The princess never did learn who this strange bird was, but watching it hang and climb, she could only laugh and dip her head.

This was the moment she'd always dreaded, and now that it had arrived, she was not afraid. In fact, she welcomed its approach.

She had at last set eyes on her enemy.

"Take heed," she said, hand on the shaft of her sword. If I die here, she realized, I will die content.

A wild recklessness seized hold of her. There was a wind blowing strong in that forest now, and its warmth filled her. She slid the sword seamlessly from its sheath. "I only wanted to see you and follow you to your lair. For you have laid waste to those whom I have loved."

The dragon snapped his fiery jaws like a dumb beast, and coals slithered down his scales and hissed as they struck the earth.

"Be warned!" said the princess. She raised her sword and thrust it in the chest of the dragon.

For a moment nothing happened.

Then the princess braced herself on one knee and yanked the sword free. The dragon vomited porridge-like globs of phlegm and stumbled, choking, into the pure, pebble-strewn stream.

The earth curved at the distant horizon. Above them both, planets spun about unknown and uncounted suns. Around the dying dragon the clean water sang while his pestilent blood seeped out and mingled with its current.

And then the dragon's body floated onto its side and slowly sank.

When the princess had cleaned her sword and returned it to her side, she looked about at the sunshine splashing through the forest. And the climbing hawk, who had broken free from the vortex and soared above her head.

Then through the magical forest came the drumbeat of hoofs, and both loyal steeds came prancing through the shafts of sunlight toward her and drew, front hoofs raised, to a stop.

"Princess?" The prince clambered from a hole in the river bank. He yawned and shook his head. "I've been asleep, I think. And I dreamed you were gone forever."

The sound of "forever" echoes through the trees.

The moon trembles, tucked snugly into the sheltering nook between two peaks. I blink at its fading light. Brooks yawns and stretches his front legs, yowling when his wound stretches too.

Hours later, I stop on the bluff, the hot sun in my face. Below me is the clearing where the river I've been following and a larger river flow together. Our cabin and cache and shed and outhouse wait, scattered on the bank, as they've waited all these years. Water flows by and the sun shines on the rocks of the gravel bar where I fished with Dad. Across the river, mountains loom with Dall sheep huddled on the outcrops, staring down at us. Beyond the visible mountains are further mountains and valleys, layer upon layer east across the territories, where bears and wolves still wander free and people rarely visit.

"We're home, Brooks. We did it."

Brooks whimpers and leans against my legs.

"You're going to sit by the stove now until you're better. And eat. Think of that. Three meals a day and hot soup between meals.'"

I take my juggling balls from my pack. Standing on the cliff before scrambling downhill, I throw them into the autumn air again and again. If I drop one, it might roll all the way to the clearing.

Before I go down, I turn to look at the way I've come. A shadow flickers through the tree trunks and is gone before I can even be sure it's there.

The footing is steep, a scramble. Concentrating, I half slide down the bluff, rocks rolling underfoot, crashing and bouncing as they fall. Brooks whimpers behind me. Reaching the bottom I dust myself off and walk along the last bit of trail and through the clearing.

I've waited to come here since I was a little girl. I've lived here in my dreams. Dad disappeared from here. Only Mom came to search. Becky and I stayed with the neighbors and didn't understand.

I hear wings flapping. The raven lands below us somewhere just out of sight.

At close range, home is not quite so intact. Shutters lie rotting on the ground, ripped from windows. The door gapes open. Across the clearing, broken dishes and pans are strewn. I walk inside. Window glass is shattered like bread crumbs all over the floor. The cookstove is on its side, along with the barrel stove for heating. Lengths of stovepipe are strewn about the cabin.

"We can't sleep here, Brooks." Panic is once again battering at my head. How many nights until Mom comes? I've lost track.

Brooks collapses at my side. His infection must be exhausting him. I will do whatever I have to do. Brooks needs rest—lots of it—warm and inside.

I start to pick up the pieces. When I hold the first broken plate in my hand, I remember breakfast many years ago.

11

Cleaning This Room

It was spring when Becky's first litter of puppies was born in the night. The litter was two pups but only one lived. She named him Chili and now he lives in the cabin, mostly by the wood-stove, an arthritic but happy grandpa. Chili was the base of her team for many years. Now Becky runs his pups and grandpups when she races.

Mom fried pancakes that morning, and when I finished devouring my share, I handstanded across the room and into the bookshelf. Paperbacks rained on my head and Dad grinned. It was spring and the river ice dropped with a bang. I thought it was the books on my head.

Returning to the brambled clearing, I lay the two pieces of the plate carefully on the grass, jigsawed together. The clearing is being taken over by rosehip and raspberry bushes. There are areas of crushed grass where a moose has been bedding under the cache. The ladder is propped against a nearby spruce tree. I lean one hand on a rung and it cracks. It needs fixing before I can climb up. After I've cleaned the cabin and made it comfortable for Brooks, I'll figure out how.

The fall sun feels warmer here in the open. Soon the sun will slide between the peaks across the river. I'm here until Mom comes, I think. I'm not walking back with Brooks like this.

Numb, I slide down to the gravel bar and chuck stones—arm drawn back and stiff out from the body—across the rushing surface of the river. Sure there's a mess, I think, but I can clean it up. Looking back, I take in the array of mountains I've spent days walking through. Very strange, I realize, mounding a few almost round rocks to juggle later. At this moment, I'm not worried.

For a few minutes the tide of panic has washed away.

This is my home; it's where I belong.

I don't clean up the clearing. I don't do more than step into the cabin and look at the mess. It can all wait. The shed, however, hasn't been touched. I slide back the bolt and open the door. Dad built it to open inward so the doorway could never be blocked by snowdrifts in a storm.

Inside is a jumble of gear: toboggan, hand-cranked washing machine Dad made from a forty-five–gallon drum, dog harnesses, fuel barrels, old stoves. A lone lump of rock salt once used for tanning hides is on the table beside mouse turds. I shove it in my pocket. It will do for a start.

Before Christmas, Dad used to hole up in here to make presents: puppets and a stage, pull toys, a rocking horse. Other times, Mom would sit by the stove and carve, but mostly she worked in the kitchen when we were playing or reading.

I make Brooks comfortable on an old sleeping bag I drag out from a discarded sled bag. Then I pry the shutters off the cabin with the hammer that still hangs on a nail just inside the door. I lean the shutters against the walls and go back inside. No room to even walk around until I've hauled out some gear. I'm sure there's a pole bed heaped with musty old blankets in the far corner, but I don't even try to reach it or the barrel stove in the opposite corner. It's enough that it's intact.

Tonight I'll camp out. I'm not ready to tackle the cabin. Whistling, I unload my pack like every other night and pitch my tent in the clearing. Slowly, the sun slips behind the rosy mountains and the moon rises. I snap off lichen from a spruce tree and kick around until my boot hits the metal grill of the old fire-pit. Split chunks of wood are scattered beside it, rotten and wet, sunk in the earth. I snap dead branches off the trees in the forest and then remember the woodpile stacked against the overhang of the cabin wall.

Chunks of dry spruce are still stacked to the roof poles. It was Becky's and my job to stack the firewood and bring it in with Dad. Because I was so little, I was rather proud of my muscles. I remember following Dad into the cabin after he'd loaded a couple of small bits on my waiting outstretched arms. Mom was carving an owl at the table. Bread steamed upside down on the counter beside a bowl of melted garlic butter.

"Strong like a moose," laughed Dad when I clattered the firewood into its box.

And I cartwheeled back out the door for more.

This time when we got outside, Dad asked me to teach him. Over and over he took a running jump with his arms outstretched and then collapsed at the moment of impact. Finally I caught his knees at the proper angle and held them up for a split second. The dogs were howling and Dad was able to shout in triumph before he once again toppled over.

He wore a red lumberjack shirt.

It's still hanging on a nail in the shed.

Behind the entrance to the dragon's cave, where the sleeping prince had lain enchanted, was the sound of a trickling stream.

The prince and princess followed that trickle, leading their steeds along the water's edge between sheer black cliffs, until the stream itself was arched with a stone entrance.

Through the entrance shone a small pond. White birds dove and planed back and forth from water to cliffs again and again during the hours of daylight. At dusk they flew in procession— long lines of birds above the many streams flowing like the spokes of a wheel—and slept under moonlight on the rocking waves of a dark deep sea.

But of this pond I cannot speak, for The Place Where the Stories Come From is silent and still and serenaded only by the great white birds winging in at dawn from the faraway sea. Still, there is a look of recognition in the eyes of those who have been there, who have breathed that air and drunk from that pond and dangled their fingers in that cool water.

When the prince and the princess rode back to the royal palace, it lay beneath a blanket of ivy. Not a bird stirred. The sun shone and bees alone droned amongst the acres of wild flowers. The prince and the princess did not speak on their return, though sometimes their gazes crossed and then moved away.

"The king is sleeping in his royal bedroom," ventured the prince as they clattered across the moat on the ancient wooden bridge. "He has been asleep since we left."

And side by side they drew up in front of the decaying palace to face what lay inside.

I kneel beside the fire-pit outside the cabin door and light a match on a rock from the circle. I hold it to the kindling and watch the flames spread first to my teepee of twigs and then to sticks and chunks of split spruce. Flames lap at the outside of the wood first, curving with the contours of the wood until each piece disintegrates, collapsing into coals and finally ash. Smoke wafts across the clearing for the first time in many years. Dad and Becky and I used to cook caribou steaks over this fire, hunkered down on our spruce stumps, while Mom was carving.

The forest is silent, like a beach when the tide has been suddenly sucked out to sea. Without warning, a wave of loneliness crashes over me. Something's choking in my throat. I stand away from the smoke and realize I'm moaning. How can I make camp? Or look for my father or clean the mess he left behind? Squatting on a chunk of upended firewood, I hunch over the flames until I can breathe slowly again.

I finish making camp and crawl into the tent, holding myself because there's no one else. Brooks whines at the door.

I've forgotten Brooks. I unzip the tent and he squeezes onto my feet. I haven't even washed his wound tonight. Nor can I force myself to move. I don't want to see the cabin.

From across the river I hear wolves calling to each other over the empty expanse of tundra beyond the trees.

They must have followed us down. Becky says wolves call partly to mark their territory.

In the morning, loosely woven mats of slush ice are floating with the current past the cabin, flowing together and sealing shut like scabs along the banks. After tea I stand in the cabin doorway. I've been home for part of a day now and a night. I remember things from yesterday: new memories are being stuck over the old.

"Dad!" I shouted. "There's an otter in the river." Dad had shaving cream on his face, and Chili, the new puppy, was sucking noisily at Ginger. "Gross!" I muttered, although I secretly believed it was beautiful.

Dad dabbed shaving cream on my nose and I stuck it back on him. I somersaulted down the bank to where Becky was calling. It was spring, and though I was too little to understand why, there was a fresh start in the air.

Brooks leans against my leg. I unhook an old parka from a nail behind the door and spread it out for him to lie on. Slowly he sinks onto it and slurps at his wound.

My throat burns from trying not to cry. Then, very clearly, the thought comes to me: there's no one here to listen.

I pick up the old broom from the corner and sweep, though a shovel would be more useful. If I live to be a great-grandma, I will only ever have one father. Only one man will ever say with pride, "My daughter did that."

And, dead or alive, he left.

"What part of that, Dad," I ask the man dabbing the shaving cream on my nose and laughing, "didn't you understand?"

I look at my hands, wrapped around the handle and tip of the broom. They're fine-boned and strong and can juggle fire. They're grown-up hands now, like my father's, not a child's, and they need to clean this room.

PART 2

The Wind
Passes
Over It

12

Pirates in the Night

As for man, his days are as grass;
As a flower of the field so he flourisheth.
For the wind passes over it, and it is gone;
And the place thereof shall know it no more.

(Psalm 103)

The words are printed in black marker on cardboard tacked behind the stove. The edges are stained and sooty. I don't know why I didn't notice it last night. Pretty weird—it doesn't sound like the Dad I remember at all. Much too serious. I tuck it inside the pages of a book and stick it on a shelf.

While the cabin light is still dim, I dissolve the salt lump in a basin of hot water and wash the pus from Brooks's side. I don't wait until the sun floods the floorboards with light. I don't want to see the wound too clearly.

While Brooks naps, I fill a tin bucket with debris from the floor and chuck it where the slop pile once spilled down the bank. Around noon I wrestle the two stoves back in place under their safeties and connect the scattered lengths of pipe. I find a couple in the shed next door to replace the most badly battered, and somehow, by the time the sun is sinking between peaks, pipe is sticking from stove holes out the roof.

I light fires in both stoves and keep shoveling out glass while the smoke clears in the cabin. I dump the broken glass in the river so animals won't slash their feet walking by the clearing. The glass should be pulverized to sand with next spring's breakup.

At dark I hammer plastic bags from my pack over window holes and light kerosene lamps. A barrel behind the cabin still contains fuel. Tomorrow I can look for real see-through window plastic. We always left some to replace any windows broken in our absence and for doubling over glass during cold snaps. I boil rice with dried onions and donate most of my portion to Brooks, who's shifted to lying beside the cookstove. I move the parka underneath him, but he barely rouses.

A wind sweeps through the clearing and moans its way downriver.

It's too dark to check out the cache. Tomorrow, I think, I'll nail green poles beside the rotting ladder rungs.

I yank tent pegs from the ground outside and spread the tent out flat over the floorboards in the kitchen, along with my travel sleeping bag and pad. I boil tea water in my camp billycan and watch the shadows in the corners of the cabin. There are no voices whispering from long ago.

The debris may be gone, but the floorboards, counters, shelves and even the ceiling need scrubbing. Strings of ancient dust mixed with spider webs hang from corners and windowsills, ready to blow in my face when I clean. In places the moss chinking between the wall logs has shriveled and fallen out.

In the night a wind grazes past the corners of the cabin and rattles the stovepipe jutting to the sky. I can't sleep. I think about reading, but it's too cold to keep my hands out of the sleeping bag to hold the book. The log walls need to warm up before they'll retain any heat. No new fairy tales come waltzing into my mind either.

What do true fairy tales need? A quest, of course, and willingly assumed danger. The landscape has to be right as well: forests and cottages in clearings and river glades, and enchanted castles covered with brambles and guarded by beasts. The main character should be brave. Beauty is optional, though it is often revered when found. There must be emotion: a quest without longing is boring. And "to quest" means "to look for."

I lie on my back and listen to the wind. Finally I sit up with my back propped against the cupboard so I can peer out the window into the night. I let my mind roam, but still no characters ride in to take charge.

I hear the river carrying tinkling cakes of slush ice and the lull of wind traveling from the peaks...

Images of my childhood reel through my mind in color and sound like they're happening before my eyes. When I was little I got excited about almost anything. Quests were all around me; it was just a matter of picking which to follow. Passion poured from every moment of my life.

In my mind, I'm tucked into the bottom bunk.

How strange that the real physical bunk is not only in my memory, where it's lain all these years, but in this actual room with me, grubby with neglect against the far wall. A squirrel has scattered moss and dried mushrooms on the mattress. I can see the bunk shadowed in the moonlight that streams through the tarp I've tucked into the empty window frame beside it.

Becky was above me, head dangling down from the top bunk. She poked me with a wooden sword she'd carved with Mom from a length of kindling. "Get up," she hissed. "We're going out."

I buried my face in the blankets and snored dramatically.

The sword tickled my cheek. I swatted at it, and it clattered to the floor. Instantly, Becky's head disappeared onto her own pillow and I heard snores coming from her too.

"Go to sleep," Dad shouted from their bedroom.

When I'd just slipped cozily back into my dreams, Becky landed with a thud on my mattress, having catapulted herself over the top bunk. I knew this without opening my eyes because it happened at least twice a night, no matter what I did. I'd tried ignoring her and kicking her. Once, when evicted from a happy dream, I even cried.

"Wolves," she mouthed. "Follow me." She handed me my own sword, waved hers in a circle over her head and thrust it bravely before her.

I was awake then. I wavered a moment between the warmth of my blankets and the waiting trial. Adventure won.

Luckily my pajamas were the toddler type with built-in feet. I followed her on tiptoe to the door, and we inched it shut behind us. Indeed, wolves were surrounding the clearing, eyes shining in the forest of moonlight. Becky clutched my hand firmly to ensure I didn't get taken away.

"Good evening, wolves," she pronounced. "You leave my little sister alone."

We struck brave poses.

"Avast, ye wolves," I told them. Pirates said it; that's all I knew.

Becky held her sword to the sky with her free hand. I wriggled out of her grasp, dropped to one knee and held my sword as far in front of that knee as possible without keeling over.

Above our heads a star plunged. For a moment it looked like it would splash into the river, but of course its light blazed out long before. I was struck speechless with happiness: the wolves, the silver moonlit sky, our smooth-handled swords and the stars embedded in the dome above.

Mom and Dad were mumbling in the cabin. I heard footsteps, the rifle being lifted from its pegs and the door opening behind us. Mom chucked blankets around our shoulders and Dad knelt on one leg with the rifle lifted at his right shoulder.

"Over their heads," said Mom.

Dad jerked the barrel up and shot into the air. Then he reached out his hand and touched Mom's hand. His fingers curled around hers. She took her spare hand and held it against his cheek. "Thanks," said Mom. "I like wolves. They're not so different from us."

Wolves wheeled back into the shadows. They milled about for a minute or two, then loped off, hunting for a less guarded meal.

Sled dogs tucked their heads deeper under their tails, curled in straw beds in their snow-buried houses.

When my family went inside, I stayed out awhile, wrapped in blankets and peace. I'd never been alone in the night before. I pretended the stars and the wolves were my friends. I pretended I'd lost my family and I was going to live with the pack. I wavered back and forth between a dead family and one that was simply lost. Never did I consider being lost myself. Maybe they were sick. Yes, that was it. My family was sick, and I was just joining the pack for a while so I could bring them back some meat. Fresh meat should heal them, I thought.

The sky was big, I realized, and our cabin and clearing were very small. Why could I only see a little way into the forest, but when I looked up I could see for light-years through the sky? I got sleepy trying to figure out what a light-year was. I thought it was the amount of light needed to light up a year of my life, but if that was true, I didn't understand how light-years could measure distance. And if I asked anyone, they'd tell me, *but they'd smile like I was cute. I hated being cute. I stood at attention, sword rigid at my side and saluted the stars.*

Then I crawled back into my bunk and curled into a ball beneath the blankets...

⁂

I don't feel better here. Why did I ever imagine that I would? If I live to be one hundred, I'll never come back, never even look at a picture of this place. If Mom or Becky mentions the bush, I'll pick up my juggling balls and try a new trick. Left to right and right to left. I'll hum under my breath.

Eventually I fall asleep again, sparks popping up the stovepipe and into the night. When I wake, my breath is steaming. Brooks is curled into my side. The cold empty cabin strums with silence. I shrug off the sleeping bag twisted around my body and stand, throwing on my sweater and tuque while I hop on sock feet to keep warm. Both stoves are frosty to the touch. I dash outside for kindling, which I've forgotten to bring inside.

Snow has fallen in the night, but the snow clouds have sailed on and the morning is clear and deep blue. Wind is playing through the tops of spruce boughs like distant surf. There are no tracks anywhere. I jump across the clearing, snap off some lichen and slide back to the door.

Brooks hasn't budged. I haul him up, arms around his stomach, until he heaves himself to his feet. "Out that door, Brooks. Time to pee."

When done, Brooks stands head down at the door and waits without whining until I let him in. He sinks back onto his bed and, I swear, he moans. His wound may be closing up but there's infection inside, maybe spreading poison through his whole body. Without an antibiotic, I can't do a thing.

All morning while the tin stove glows cherry red, I heat tubs of water and wash as many surfaces as I can. Steam fills the cabin with a smell like moldy socks, but I don't care. I use old childhood clothes for rags and throw them in a heap out the door to burn in a blaze outside later. If I had a radio, like Mom begged me to take, I'd call in a chopper this morning. "I'm fine myself," I'd say. "No problems with me. But my dog needs to see a vet."

I need a voice, any voice that's not my own and not in the past. I find a roll of window plastic and tack pieces over the window holes. Mountains aren't peaceful like I always thought. They're only big, and they go on forever here: it's wild from one side of the continent to the other and then comes the ocean. And the landscape will go on, changing only over the centuries of geological time, long after everyone I love is dead.

"Don't die, Brooks," I beg, kneeling at his side. His ribs are visible, stomach collapsing. The silence after his final breath will last forever. Brooks's tail sweeps the floor, but he doesn't get up. He's tired, I think. He's moving on. Brooks doesn't care anymore. All he wants is my companionship and to stay warm.

I scrub the floorboards first, then the shelves. The counter is worn smooth from years of Mom's kneading bread, usually with one of us battering a lump by her side. I see a line of caribou trudging single file in each other's tracks up the bowl of a mountain across the river. Snow melts, dripping from the roof, and the ground emerges again. I move Brooks's bed into the sunshine and force him out so he feels the fresh air.

By afternoon the sun is shining and the river is ice-free. I throw the last of the wash water onto the slop pile and stare down the valley, swinging the empty bucket. Silence murmurs in my ears. Then, very slowly, sound washes back: a chattering squirrel clings to a tree trunk, a black-capped chickadee lands on a shivering branch with feathers plumped, a gray dipper bobs at the edge of the open current downriver, fishing for bugs.

Where exactly did I think Dad would be?

Brooks snores behind me; a great wave of contentment peaks from nowhere and crashes over my head. Right now, at this very moment, I still have Brooks and the mountains, and Mom and Becky, even though they're not with me.

Astounded, I slide my eyes over the mountains we walked by to get here. Not once did I get lost or turn back.

I did it, I think. I got us here; I got us back home, all the way from planning to prying off the shutters to cleaning up the rooms. No matter what happens from here, I came home when I decided to do so.

It's something, I guess. The feeling doesn't last, of course, but I had that moment and I'll remember it long after it's gone.

Long after Brooks is gone.

13

The Grayling Corral

Fresh food could help Brooks heal faster. My eyes scan the river where the grayling run should be happening soon. Every year around this time, grayling migrate to the big rivers like the Peel, where water doesn't freeze quite to the bottom. I should be able to feed Brooks and me without much work if I get on to it fast, before they're all gone. I'll catch a few grayling and then fix the cache ladder, I decide.

I force myself to wash Brooks's wound before I go fishing. Examining it at close quarters makes me retch. Crouched over the slop bucket, I vomit until I have dry heaves and my eyes water. Then I splash cold water over my face, gargle with river water and get on with it.

I pour water from the hissing kettle and mix in some cold, then dab for a while at the pus with the last of the salty brew. I don't know if it's my imagination, but there seems to be more pus now, more dead tissue and blood cells around the cut.

I grab Dad's rod from the spikes behind the door, kiss Brooks's soft twitching ears and his nose, and pull on Dad's hip waders.

Yuck!

I peel them off and tip them upside down fast onto the ground of the clearing. Years of accumulated mouse gatherings and poop slide out. I slip them back on anyway. Then I slide down the bank to catch us some fish.

I can almost smell them sizzling in the pan. Brooks will nuzzle against my legs and bay with hunger.

From the gravel bar, I can see the cache ladder leaning against a nearby spruce. The cache itself is still upright, tin on pole legs, a treehouse with a pole and plastic roof, sheltering gear up in the air from passing bears and other scavengers.

Tomorrow I'll climb up and check for my fairy-tale collection. Maybe tonight if I get the rungs replaced in time. Even if the grayling take off soon, there should still be leftover dog food from our team.

It'll be easier than looking for Dad.

I wade into the current and brace myself with legs apart at the same spot where I fished as a little girl. The water breaks around me.

Not a nibble even.

The grayling must already be gone.

My arm remembers swinging back, and then watching the curve of line dancing above the water. Again and again. I'm about to reel in for the day when I catch one, then a second. I wriggle the hooks from their mouths while the fish rock their slippery bodies, head to tail, against the icy stones.

A raven flaps over my head and lands on a rock close by. Down the valley a golden eagle circles above the river.

Kneeling, I smash the first fish's head with a stick. I'm pinning the second fish's shiny belly with my foot, stone poised over my shoulder, when I notice something. A dam built from stacked stones cuts across a dip in the gravel bar, creating a tub-sized pond. The edges are frozen, but a deep pool in the center remains ice-free.

I was wearing a T-shirt, underpants and rubber boots. A ripped T-shirt of Dad's hung on Becky like a tomato-colored sack. Mom's spaghetti strainer was wired to a pole. Becky was wading in the pond, her shirt tucked into a pair of Dad's hip waders, corralling our captive grayling from where they huddled together, noses into the current. She towed them triumphantly in the strainer around the pond and then released them in a heap. They bolted, fins flickering, and hovered motionless against the dam.

"RUN!" she ordered. "The water's leaking out."

Panicked, I plugged holes with stones until the sun slipped behind the mountains across the river.

"HURRY!" Becky shouted at intervals when I slowed. "They'll die."

My knees were bleeding. My knuckles were bruised. I was entirely soaked and hungry and desperately worried about Scales, Eddy, Berries, Currants and Easy.

Becky clambered out of the water. She shook each leg in turn until the water poured out the top of the hip waders. Then she kicked them off. Her legs looked like no legs I'd ever seen before, the color of pickled beets set on fire.

"They leak something fierce," she remarked. "Makes them heavy as rocks. Good thing I'm tough."

I was still trudging along the gravel bank with stones clutched to my heart. I, unfortunately, was not so tough. I wanted to cry with exhaustion but my sister would have been ashamed.

"Time to quit," she called cheerfully. "I smell supper."

"What about our fish? The water's still leaking out."

"Sure is," said my sister, staring at her now bare toes. "But it's also leaking in."

I let the last rock drop into place and surveyed our handiwork. Five tame fish wrestled from the wild currents of the river. We should be proud, I thought, of giving those fish a safe home. "Becky," I pronounced, "I'm never going to eat our fish."

And we never did. But before the river froze, Dad lent us a bucket and we scooped them all together like one happy family, kissed their slimy noses and upended the bucket so the fish could swim gently out without being dumped.

"Swim, little fish," I whispered.

*Becky called an encouraging good-bye to each in turn.
"On Scales! On Eddy! On Berries, on Currants, on Easy!"*

*When we climbed the bank to the clearing, I turned one last
time and saluted the vanished fish. "Be brave, little fish," I told
them. "Swim fast and swim far. And one day swim home."*

I carry the flopping second fish over to the pond and slip
it in. Fresh fish for Brooks in a day or two if I can't catch
more, I tell myself.

"Good night, Flicker," I call back, climbing the bank.
"I'll catch you some friends tomorrow."

I shove my tent back in my pack, sweep off the boards
of my old bed, stick a mattress on it and curl up. I have
a lot to do tomorrow: fishing, the cache, washing shelves
and cupboards, soaking Brooks's wound, maybe...Salt!
I should have fixed the cache and checked up there already.
Trouble is, of course, that I'm not ready to look at all our
gear, soaked with memories.

In the morning, heavy gray snow clouds have bunched
down the river valley. I need to check out trails for clues
now, before the snow stays. But Brooks needs fresh food.

Nah, I think, peering from my doorway and sipping a
hot mug of tea. The first snow usually melts. And even if it
doesn't, there won't be enough snow to cover anything.

Brooks barely reacts when I bend down to stroke his
head. His tail sweeps feebly against the floorboards.

I catch two more grayling, a mug of coffee balanced on the gravel beside me. I walk over to the pond with one I name Friend. Even the air here is more alive. I breathe in great breaths with the fish flapping in my arms.

The pond is freezing from the outside in. No way can they live in there any longer. I scoop up both fish and release them back in the river. The pond may be solid ice by morning. It's too late in life to start killing off pets, I think. The rule, though ridiculous, is not to eat anything we've named.

Sighing, I gut the lone unnamed fish on the gravel bar and boil it up at the cabin for Brooks.

It's time.

While the soup cools, I saw lengths of ladder rungs from a young spruce, lay the ladder flat on the ground and nail the new rungs into place right on top of the old ones.

After slurping warm fish broth with some enthusiasm, Brooks seems spry enough to limp after me all the way to the foot of the cache, where I heave the ladder back into position and climb.

One misstep and I could crash to the ground with no one to help me. With each step I make sure my hands firmly grip the sides of the ladder. I've climbed this ladder countless times, but Dad's hands were always just below mine.

At the top, I distribute my weight on the creaking cache porch by lying on my stomach. Below is spread an endless mosaic of mountains and rivers, strangely patterned with slush ice hissing as it drifts into eddies and then slows.

Bags of old coats, pants, sweaters and sheets. Boxes of books and cans of tomatoes, two suitcases full of spices and baking goods. Several taped and tied boxes feel like they might contain staples: one of rice, one of flour and one of noodles. After much poking, I toss those to the side to open when I have a knife. No sacks of dog food.

And worst of all: no salt. I banish the realization from my mind instantly.

A tent stove, however, is stuffed with strips of dry meat. I throw it down for Brooks. Protein will have to do.

"Should we put it on the toboggan?" asked Mom.

Piles of books teetered all over the cabin floor. She held the Irish fairy-tale book in one hand, open to an illustration of a handsome prince peering up from the bottom of a glass hill to the princess's castle.

I snatched the book from her and cradled it in my arms.

"Town or cache?" asked Mom, stuffing the books into boxes. "How did we get so many books in here anyway?"

"Cache," I decided. "That way it will always be here."

Mom tossed me a daypack. "Would this work for packing it?"

I climbed onto a stool and penciled a note in case intruders decided to stop by and raid our cache. This is the best book in the world, *I wrote, carefully thinking through the spelling of each word.* Do not steel this book!

Becky, wandering through, added a skull and crossbones and signed the note Terror of the Sea, *which I found deeply insulting. I realized she was trying to be helpful, but it wasn't her book. We folded the note into an envelope we made and sealed it shut with a dripping candle. Then I stuffed note and book in the pack, wrapped the pack in a garbage bag and handed it over to Mom.*

And there it is—right by the door all these years later—dry and safe in its plastic bag within a daypack all on its own. I breathe in the smell of its cardboard cover: *Irish Fairy Tales*. I hold it in both gloved hands and grin.

The cache sways in a gust. A pole beneath me on the cache floor snaps. I stop breathing until the cache is still.

It's time to head down. I creep slowly out on all fours, nauseous with adrenaline. The poles are probably all rotten.

I position myself with both legs on separate rungs before I let go of the cache porch, book bag clenched in my teeth. My younger self would be proud. Back on solid ground, I hump in the dry meat and a suitcase of old food. Only then do I fetch my book.

I read for the rest of the day with feet propped up on a chair beside the cookstove, pouring tea and boiling dry-vegetable-and-jerky soup. When Brooks starts to get restless right before dark, moaning and tearing at his wound,

I slip on the hip waders and step into the clearing of my magical kingdom. Then I slide down the bank to the gravel bar and wade into the current, hoping for a fresh fish dinner for him.

Not a chance. Ice is floating in to shore now. It was stupid to let those grayling free. I was counting on there being salt somewhere in our gear.

"Tomorrow I'll check out the rest of the cache," I promise Brooks as I pour the last of my soup into this morning's leftover fish broth. "I'll shake out every bag of clothes, every sheet and book. There's got to be salt somewhere."

The stench of rotting meat blasts into my face. "Yuck. We're advertising for a bear to visit by boiling fish in here."

Brooks stretches on the warm floor and falls back asleep.

Then I understand.

It isn't just the fish I smell. It's Brooks's wound. I've neglected Brooks's wound.

14

Wounds

My face is buried in the folds of Brooks's neck, my arms sealed about him. Logs settle in the stove, and a north wind rustles through the spruce boughs. We lie like that for a long, long time. In the end, Brooks staggers to his feet and stands, head bowed, by the cookstove, legs splayed, whimpering.

Water. I pour warm water into the basin and break open a sterile cloth Mom threw in my pack when I wasn't looking. I rinse the empty salt shaker with boiling water and shake it until any salt crystals clinging to its sides are dissolved. Then I make Brooks lie down on Dad's old parka and dribble water into the wound. I don't let him get up even when he tries to nip me when the water washes the pus away.

"Forget it, boy," I tell him, playing with his ears.

I need more water. Bucket in hand, I walk down to the gravel bar, the cabin behind me, and above me a smudge of lamplight from the plastic windows. The sky is salted with coarse stars, and the northern lights open and close like green and red accordions above the mountain peaks. The temperature is dropping by the minute while the moon rocks between racing clouds. The wall of spruce trees bends and straightens in chorus as the wind soughs through their boughs and hurtles on across the still river. Cakes of ice have formed and are banging down the current. Brooks might die because I came looking for Dad.

I wander farther down the gravel bar to where the creek I followed to get here joins the creek flowing through the main valley. This too has frozen out from the bank. The moon peeks out long enough for me to see what must have been made days ago when the ground was still soft enough to take an imprint.

A line of tracks, like a barefoot human's, cuts along the gravel bar. By the shore, where ice meets rock, the tracks take several detours out. I can see where the shore ice has broken and the bear has leapt back almost as if he was playing.

Could the bear have followed us here?

I stand on the shelf ice and chop a hole for my bucket. Every few chops I swivel around fast to check behind me. Clouds cover the moon and stars, and the northern lights fade away. The wind is calm now from the mountain passes. Even the slush of moving ice is still.

Only my cabin is still lamp-lit in the black expanse of forest and tundra.

I pick four round stones from my heap and juggle, slowly warming up to my latest trick. Instead of catching the balls, I snatch them from above as they drop. It's an easy trick for an audience to follow but still fluid and beautiful.

Brooks, I'm so sorry. I haven't been worried enough about you. I've been mourning for a long-gone father while you decayed before my eyes.

Stars blink into place above me. Mourning isn't the right word anymore. For years I remembered little more than Dad leaving. Now whole scenes are washing up in my memory. I relax and scavenge through them.

Our campfire was spitting head-high flames into a sky heavy with stars. Dad chucked on another log and shoved a stump at me.

"Have a seat," he laughed. "Make yourself comfortable."

Huddled close to the flames, I peeled a willow with my knife and threaded on a chunk of caribou meat. "Want some?"

"Sure," he said. "I'll get some boughs."

It was just Dad and me breaking trail, sleeping in the snow with a tarp as a backdrop for the campfire. That night we slept on spruce boughs topped with caribou hides and down sleeping bags. I didn't take off my parka until the bag was thoroughly warmed up. Every so often Dad threw spruce on the fire from a pile he'd stacked within reach. I didn't tell him, but I was making up a story about the stars. Certain stars were friendly, and they were about to have a celebration—maybe Christmas—with other constellations. It was kind of pathetic, but stars were like my toys; they had personalities and I couldn't wait to see them come out.

"Asleep, Rachel?"

"Maybe."

"Cold?"

"Course not."

Who could be cold when they're winter camping with their dad? Even if they were shaking with misery, who would SAY it?

"You sound cold."

I sat up in my sleeping bag, tuque pulled down almost to my eyes. I pointed at the campfire. Around its heat, bare earth was emerging: moss, leaf litter, wizened flower stalks.

"It's growing summer," I said.

"We'll take some moss with us," said Dad, placing a couple of split chunks on the flames.

"What for?"

"It's an antibiotic. People used it for treating wounds. And it's hard to gather once there's snow."

"Once me and Becky made pussy willows," I said, mittened hands behind my head so I could enjoy the view.

There was a pause, long enough that I knew Dad was trying to tell me to get to sleep. Or, at least, that he'd like to himself.

"How?" he mumbled.

"In the fire-pit last Christmas. We burned a fire there so hot that the willows we had in the pile thought it was spring."

This was the most remarkable bit of information I knew. Becky and I fooled willows into believing it was spring.

Dad, however, grunted and disappeared inside his bag.

The next thing I knew, the stars were fainter and a pot of hot water was hissing on coals raked to one side. Dad was cross-legged by the flames, rummaging in the sled bag for tea. The too-loud crackling of the sled bag told me the temperature had dropped in the night.

"Do you like fairy tales?" I asked him.

"Love them," said Dad. "Can't tell you why, but I always have."

I shake my head as I slosh the water in the bucket.

Moss is a natural antibiotic. How could I have forgotten?

Surely the starlight's bright enough to search for some right now. I grab the ax to chop a frozen slab, thick on the side of a rotting stump.

Brooks's tail thumps, brushing the floorboards, when I shoulder in with clumps of moss and ice. His head barely lifts from the floor, but his eyes follow my every move.

The past wasn't sad at all; it was pretty damn happy. I wash his wound until it is white around its edge, with no pus.

I don't know how to use the moss. If I get it wrong, there's a good chance Brooks will die.

First I boil a handful in a small amount of water with the lid on to keep in the active medicinal parts. After it has cooled, I pour the moss and broth over the wound like a seaweed soup and bind it with a shirt. While the wound is steeping, I prop up my feet and read fairy tales to Brooks: "The Snow Queen" is his favorite, I decide, because he chooses, when Kay's splinter of ice dissolves, to actually lumber to his feet and whine at the door. Either that or he has to go pee.

I keep close watch through the window all the time Brooks is outside to make sure the bear's not around. I pretend a prince is camping a few miles from here. Tomorrow I'll be chopping wood and I'll stop, amazed, with the ax behind my head, and slowly lower it when the prince comes into view.

The bear must have been up for one last stroll before hibernating. Would he still be wandering around in this cold?

Steam rises from downriver. Mist fingers the bank and flows across the clearing.

When Brooks whimpers to be let in, I place thawed and moistened moss over the cut and tie another bandage around it. The bandage is an old T-shirt of Dad's that was lying around. There's nothing sterile left but it's not touching the wound anyway.

Tomorrow I'll boil up a bunch of our childhood shirts.

"Come on, Brooks," I coax my hound. "Let's get to bed." I need to be right there if he gets any worse, so he won't feel abandoned. I load the barrel stove for the first time for night burning: round chunks that will smolder through the darkness. I've never used a chain saw before, I realize, though I watched Mom and Dad countless times. Unless I can figure it out, I'll be swede-sawing my wood while I'm here. That's how I'll be spending my days, cutting into tree trunks, limbing branches, heaving logs onto my shoulder and staggering home with them.

I bend with my knees and grab Brooks. It takes all my strength to carry him to the bed and lift him up, moss and bandages still tied in place. "Night, pup," I say, kissing his floppy ears and hopping into bed myself. "See you in the morning."

In the morning Brooks is still warm. I touch his fur before I dare open my eyes. He staggers outside to pee and stands, head down, outside the door without even lifting his hind leg until I let him back in to sleep. Fear tears at me, churning my stomach and scrambling my thoughts.

Snow has fallen steadily throughout the night onto the frozen ground. I blink outside in the brightness. I have to search the trails for Dad now before they're covered. Today.

First I wash Brooks with the moss-water again and tie up the steeping wound with a boiled bandage. There's nothing else I can do for him. I leave him curled, head under tail, on a bag by the loaded stove. Strange how having my dog fills the cabin even when I'm outside. Without him, there'd be no one to return for, no one to take care of or share my days with.

Before I leave I check the cache again, this time laying two long poles at right angles to the porch poles to take the pressure off the rotten wood. I stay prone with the fresh poles directly under my stomach.

I check each container thoroughly, finding flour, oats, oil, beans, brown sugar, a sack of ancient baking supplies, some breast-shaped containers of Real Lemon to ward off scurvy.

But still no salt. I don't think about that; the moss has to work. And we should be fine for food. There's even a half-full can of cocoa. Tonight I'll bake a cake. Nah, chocolate makes dogs sick. I'll make lemon spice cake with brown sugar and coconut icing broiled on top. Brooks could do with the extra energy.

I throw it all down the ladder and leave it sitting in the snow to deal with when I return.

That was a mistake.

Nah, it was nothing short of stupid.

Clues

Trouble is, I haven't really thought through how I will search for him. How do you look for a man who's been missing for so many years?

I walk downriver, letting my mind wander, the river bearing its slush to my right, spruce and cottonwood forest to my left. Beyond both, white mountains climb to a pale clear sky. The sun rises halfheartedly and throws no heat anymore. My feet know this trail still. Dad's blazes are on tree trunks every couple of minutes but animals have kept the trail open since we left: moose, wolves and foxes, probably even caribou and sheep, crossing the valley in the summer for a mineral lick.

I walk for miles, over a frozen slough and farther into the trees and through a tangle of willow crossed with rabbit tracks. I walk past the cutoff to the beaver pond and see no fresh blazes, no smoke or hidden cabins: no clues.

On the way back I head down the trail to the beaver pond. The fire should be still smoldering. Brooks will be toasty beside it, and besides, he needs the sleep.

I sat on a pile of spruce boughs that Dad had chopped and I'd piled for warmth. Beside me, Dad was cross-legged, leaning against a trunk. I fidgeted with twigs and pebbles, making up stories. I was bored but I would have cut out my heart before I'd mention it. Becky was off for a day with Mom and the dogs somewhere, and I was home alone with Dad. Course, home alone with Dad meant hardly being home. We were spending the evening beaver hunting.

It was spring and the pond was open and the caribou were wandering and the wolves were frisking about in the still-dark nights. We heard them at night from all directions. Maybe they met up with packs that had broken off from theirs, Dad said. Like getting the whole family together for a spring reunion. Thing is, nobody knows much about how wolves behave in the wild.

The snow was good for snowballs finally. It packed together, wet from the sun melting it during the day. At nights, of course, the land froze tight and the snow grew a brittle surface layer of ice.

Dad poked me.

At the beaver pond, a baby beaver was swimming. I saw the flat brown head and the streamlined, curious body paddling toward us. A large beaver surfaced beside me and slapped its tail hard on the water. The larger beaver dove but the baby swam on toward us.

Dad held his rifle to his shoulder.

"No."

He leaned it against the next tree trunk and held up his arms in surrender.

"I wasn't going to shoot. Matter of fact, I'm not taking any more beaver this spring."

And he didn't.

Every evening we sat by the pond, sometimes with Becky and Mom, and had picnics with bannock and meat roasted on green willow sticks over a small blaze. After several nights of this, the beavers began to ignore us, and when Becky brought her dogs down, the beavers teased them by swimming close to shore, slapping their tails and diving.

"They're so weird," Becky said. "If someone told me about beavers, I wouldn't believe a word of it. Little animals that design their own pools. They're engineers!"

Becky was fascinated by animals; that's why she's so good at running dogs. But I just wanted to hang out with Dad.

I walk through the trees, and there's the pond with the dam and the feed pile of mounded sticks and the beaver house.

The beavers must be sleeping on ledges underwater. Fallen cottonwood with fresh beaver-teeth marks lie about. I march around the pond for a while, looking for our old spruce bough heaps, but they've long ago lost their needles and rotted into the general leaf debris. There's no sign we were ever here.

And there's no sign of Dad anywhere.

At least there's fresh beaver sign.

On the way back, I find a black comb lying across the trail. Mom doesn't use combs, just brushes. Running my fingers along the teeth, I feel the slip of mold. It may have lain there for years but I carry it carefully to the cabin anyway. Broken prongs stab into the palm of my hand.

I see smoke flying like a flag from the stovepipe while I'm still in the forest.

Brooks barks from inside when he hears me, and something heavy slips from my shoulders in relief. He's at the door before I am, pushing into my legs and slipping past me into the clearing. He even yaps as he chases his tail briefly before going back inside.

He still smells putrid.

But the wound, when I stare at it, seems perhaps a bit cleaner, a little less inflamed. I almost dare to hope.

For the first time, I let myself imagine the clearing with Brooks's body cold by the stove. My mind skitters from the picture, and I whistle him back in to rest. All the time I'm frying bannock, I keep up a running stream of talk—about the trail, the beavers, the moldy comb. Before bed,

I chop a box of frozen moss and leave it to thaw beside the stove. I soak Brooks's cut with moss soup and bandage it with a fresh wet poultice.

That night Brooks is restless, whining by the door and pacing in the kitchen from window to window. Bare feet on the table, I read my fairy-tale book by the stove: "The Snow Queen" again. Greta, still chasing her lost friend across the steppes and taiga, is in an ice palace filled with thieves.

Brooks barks, a paw lifted, a series of alarm calls. I check out the window and, sure enough, a black wolf is standing in the clearing staring toward the cabin, head lowered slightly and eyes shining. I pull on wool socks and step into my boots. The moon is over the river and shining on the fresh snow, and snow is thumping softly from spruce branches in the wall of forest. I hear a keening from the trees to the right and see shadows moving. As I watch, seven long-legged wolves step out, form a semi-circle in full view and howl.

Brooks dives under our bed so only his nose sticks out.

Then I realize what I've done. In the moonlight, scattered heaps are visible beneath the cache. I've forgotten to bring in the food. Snow streams in the wind, flat above the ground like schools of small fish darting back and forth.

I carry the lamp to the counter so it throws light out the window, shrug into Dad's red lumberjack shirt and lift his rifle from its pegs behind the door. I break open the chamber, blow through the barrel and load it.

Holding it at hip level, cowboy style, I stalk backward across the clearing, away from the wolves. Wolf eyes lock onto mine. Ice clangs in the current. The neighborhood raven flies over the wolves and disappears somewhere in the trees.

Once beneath the cache, I load my pack by feel, never moving gun barrel or eyes from my visitors. And above us all, the northern lights stroll onto their stage, filling the valley with wild flings of green and white light, like sheets snapping across the heavens.

Dad used to pee on the ground beside any meat he had to leave out overnight. It was his form of scent marking and it seemed to actually work; interspecies communication, he told me, smug. I'm laughing. The wolves are silent now, heads still slightly bowed. They begin to walk away into the forest, floating on their endless legs.

The first wolf, the blackest and biggest, stays the longest, muzzle quivering. Alone he howls, a drawn-out note to his pack, breaking pitch once at the beginning and once at the end. As he calls, his nose lifts slightly to the sky and I see his breath steaming in the cooling night. From the surrounding forest, wolves sing back. I turn my head slightly to hear. Each wolf is howling in its own separate pitch. Ice swishes its way along the river on a higher note. Upriver, ice cracks like a drumroll, fast and deep.

Pack full, I stand and howl along, chanting the word *keen* but letting the *e* sound linger in the night. I can smell the wolf now, and the smoke drifting across the clearing and the dried vegetable soup I boiled for my boring dinner. I can smell the cold air blowing softly from the mountain passes, brushing at the skin of my face. The blue moonlight is almost as bright as the middle of a winter day.

I lower the rifle. I walk back past the black wolf to the cabin door with my father's gun dangling by my side and a pack full of ancient, probably moldy, food on my back. As I get close, the wolf draws back and runs into the shadows to join his pack. Wolves don't hurt people anyway, at least almost never. It's mostly Brooks I'm worried about.

"Liar!" I say out loud, and, startled, I laugh. The sound is weird in the dark.

Branches crack as the pack lopes away. From a distance, they howl and pause and howl again. I can't tell where the song is coming from.

Brooks is getting better. In that moment I know it.

I've never been so happy. Happiness wells inside me and makes me sing.

That's what happiness feels like, I think: the need to sing.

16

Undercurrents

Brooks sits, head cocked to the side, staring at me and licking his muzzle, a ridiculous blend of husky fur and hound ears and loose folds of skin on his face. "Not bad, eh?" I jam the rifle against my shoulder and shoot again. A puff of snow falls from the stump I'm shooting at. "Always was a good shot, Brooks."

Brooks yawns and stretches his front legs.

I stand, brushing snow off my red lumberjack shirt and wool pants. Dad's actually; I found them in the cache. Every day I hump a box down the ladder and drag it into the cabin to sift through at night. Brooks dives through the snow, digging a trough with his long nose. I lean the gun against a trunk and hug him. I'm not taking any chances. "I'm soaking your cut again tonight," I tell him, "and you'd better keep it clean."

Brooks is running, nose to a rabbit's tracks. The raven lands on a spruce branch, dislodging snow, and *acks* at us loudly. Ice is barely flowing now. Soon the river will be solid ice.

The raven flaps low to the ground in front of Brooks to get his attention. Ravens live so long they must get bored with the regular turn of the seasons. Amusement can be in short supply in the bush. The raven dives at Brooks's tail and at the last moment flies up with a great flapping of black wings. I stare. I don't believe this raven.

Warm air hums and strums its way above the trees and wafts through the clearing. I wrinkle my nose and breathe in great draughts of spruce needles and Labrador tea and willow and a more robust flavor, like caribou, just a hint. "Lunch, Brooks."

I leave the door open so the wind plays through the cabin. I stand beside the cherry red cookstove with the fresh air blowing on my bare head as I fry bannock. Drops of ancient grease fly from the pan and ping on the metal, stinging my eyes with smoke.

When it's golden and crunchy, I chuck the bannock from hand to hand to cool. Then I spread it with Mom's cranberry jam that I've thawed above the stove all night. I bet I helped her pick the berries. Probably we all did: long family days in the fall with the sun lower and lower each day and finally not rising at all, and the five-gallon buckets humped in our small hands when we refused to give them up.

I remember Dad singing old hobo songs and Mom, giving up on berries, carving against a tree trunk while the rest of us picked. And I remember the feel of sunshine on my face and the smell of cranberries and the mingling odors of leaf litter pressing against my nose. I used to squint my eyes shut and sniff. Mom's hair smelled like sunshine when I leaned against her shoulder.

Sometimes Dad dropped beside her and they hugged. Then he would pull me close to them and poke me, and I'd laugh and wander off to play with Becky.

I throw Brooks half the bannock and wolf the rest down, leaning against the open doorway. The warm weather should blow away by night, but it's relaxing now. The river is empty of fish for the winter. Snowshoe hares don't need trails yet; the snow isn't deep enough. They can still run wherever they like. There's no point in setting snares in the forest, but later I will.

The raven lands with fluffed feathers and bobs his head, hopping across the snow. "Fine," I laugh, and chuck him a burnt bit. He flaps off with bannock in beak, and a while later I see him circling above the river. You take your friends where you can find them here.

And then it's night again. It comes so early now that I'm restless. Leaving Brooks on the parka so he's cozy, I stroll downriver again, Dad's rifle in hand to make me feel safer. As backup, I keep a can of bear spray tucked in my inside parka pocket so it won't freeze.

I can't smell the forest carried on currents of warm wind anymore. Above me, the moon and a million stars shine and bounce light from the skiff of snow. I see marten tracks and scattered three-point rabbit tracks and high-bush cranberry laden with red berries. I pick a handful and let them thaw in my mouth.

I wander for miles, without thinking much, while the moon travels above the mountains and the northern lights jig above the black horizon. I try the new shelf ice for a while, but I'm nervous, ears straining for a crack. Breaking off a dead spruce pole, I plant it hard into the ice before each step. The stick thuds safely. Really, using it is just slowing me down.

Without warning, the pole breaks through. Cracks spread like spider webs across the fresh ice.

I jump back as the current snatches the pole from my hands. It hesitates, bobbing at the far lip of the hole, before it is sucked under. Adrenaline swarms through my whole body like a hive of bees. Ice shifts under my feet. Cracks boomerang. The whole system is breaking up. I walk heel to toe backward, Dad's rifle over my shoulder. Scrambling up the bank, I hear myself panting.

Without the pole I would be under the ice.

I imagine myself carried by the current under the ice, trying to shoot through a moonlit hole. I'd catch a glimpse of night sky and then a ceiling of ice as I hurtled by.

Worse, I can picture it happening to Dad. I'd never know.

The warm cabin and tea sound pretty appealing. I make for home and Brooks, following in my old footsteps.

If I'd gone under, Brooks would probably have died of thirst in the cabin.

There's no lamplight shining through the clearing, but I creak open the door. Not a sound except a breeze playing in the stovepipe.

"Brooks?"

Brooks jumps from a deep sleep and wanders over to nuzzle and push against my legs. I grope for the matches on the table and light the lamp; the soft yellow light shines on us both. From the safety ring on the stove, a faint red glow peeks out, and I open it and shove in more wood and shoulder off my outdoor clothes. Through the open doorway a silver-blue bar of moonlight fingers the floorboards.

I close the door and hug Brooks against my legs so I can play with his ears. Then I pour warm water from the kettle into the washbasin and get him to lie on his side. Cloth poised, I realize the wound has sealed. I lay warm compresses steeped in moss tea over the wound awhile until it softens. No pus beads along the scar. Nor does Brooks flinch.

"I love you, puppy," I whisper in sheer relief that we're both alive. "Maybe tomorrow you can come too. But we'll stay off the ice."

That night I sleep with my arm around Brooks and no bad dreams seep in, though the stove flares up and I wake to the play of firelight reflected on the log walls and have to throw water in the stove. A blast of smoke chokes me, and I open the door and stare out into the night. Far off I hear the wolves howling their individual notes. A sudden gust of wind shakes the ice floes in the river. They shudder and crash, rearing against each other. I shiver and watch a star falling through the sky.

Then I shove more chunks of wood on the tamed fire and crawl back into bed. And again I sleep without dreams and wake hungry to a snow-bright day.

17

The Snow Queen

"Of course we could live on oats and flour and rice until Mom gets here," I say. Brooks sits, licking his lips as he waits for me to hand over my breakfast. Saliva trails from the corner of his mouth. I'm ravenous. Maybe I'll give him the bowl to lick. "But I'd love to get some fresh meat."

Later I walk, with Brooks at heel, down the only trail we can use until the rivers freeze solid. Every hundred feet, we stop and scan the horizon and the mountainsides, and then I peer through the low, wild, gray forest. I watch particularly for movement, not just of animals themselves but also of branches they may have brushed. Then I scan once again for anything sticking out, too much regularity or an unusual shade. Before moving again, Brooks breathes in a great symphony of smells, a tapestry of wild scents. I sniff beside him, pulling air through my nostrils until my lungs feel full. Brooks moves, head down, sniffing tracks. Once, I lie on my stomach and close my eyes, breathing hard next to a rabbit track.

Nothing. Maybe humans had hunter noses at one time, but we haven't needed them for centuries.

Do blind people develop a more acute sense of smell as well as hearing?

I walk on, noting where the river still flows some places in an open channel and some places over top of ice that is surging beneath the surface. Details are sharper in the cold air today; spruce needles on boughs and leftover birds' nests in the crotch of willow branches stand out as if seen through my monocle. Back home, both stoves are full and the cache ladder is leaning against a nearby spruce tree so I can lift it easily back into place, but no passing creatures can climb into the cache. A kettle of water is hissing at the far edge of the cookstove so it will stay hot but not boil. A box of wooden matches, decorated with an eagle in flight, lies on the table where I can grope for it even after dark.

Loose matches are in my coat pocket too. At the point where we decide to return, I pull one out and strike the sulfur tip against a rock on a gravel bar where we once camped. I break off old-man's beard and crumple it into a heap, hold the match to the pile and blow. Flames catch the lichen and then twigs and branches.

I pick the roundest rocks and juggle. In gloves, the rocks feel different. I need to concentrate more. I keep up a regular cascade until the fire is burning smoothly with driftwood.

I try the "snatching from above" trick and the "behind the back." Not enough flexibility with a coat so I shrug it off, stoking the fire even higher.

Before leaving, I push three straight sticks into the flames so only the ends catch fire. I pull them out, fire licking down the wood, and throw the torches toward the sky. I hear the *whoosh* of flame each time a stick flies. There's a second when the fire is directly above my face. I force myself not to blink, and then their fire goes out.

I keep juggling with the charred sticks—obviously there must be a better way to keep them lit. Brooks curls by the fire and sleeps. I juggle until my feet, stuck in home position, begin to stab from cold. Then I chuck my torches on the bonfire. No need to douse the flames on a gravel bar with the snow falling.

Snow is falling in fat soft flakes that fill the sky, dancing like dust motes through a window.

On the way home I notice them.

Over my tracks, over Brooks's tracks is another set of bear prints. The bear followed us downriver. He must have been standing in the shadows while I juggled. He was watching from the snow and Brooks didn't even catch his scent. I cup my hands around my mouth and yodel loudly in the direction the tracks have taken. "Leave us alone, bear," I say. "That's enough."

I'm starving when I get back to the cabin. I devour a spoonful of brown sugar, grain by grain, while I wait for porridge to boil: dry flakes turning to mush and spluttering to the surface only to be dragged down again into the bowels of the pot. I share with Brooks, even though I'd rather not. Hunger tears at my stomach. I drink cup after cup of black tea and read "The Snow Queen" out loud to make it last.

I've been forgetting about fairy tales. I read a page and lick my finger to turn it over, holding the book close to my face. I smell faint traces of must from the years the book lay in the cache while the winds from the passes blew through the open spaces between its log walls.

"The Snow Queen" is about a young girl, Greta, whose dearest friend, a boy named Kay, wanders off with the Snow Queen because he has a magic sliver of ice in his heart that makes him hard and cruel. None of this is his fault, Greta is sure. It's the Snow Queen's way of casting a spell.

Greta, of course, goes taking off in pursuit of Kay.

An old woman in a wooden cottage built into a hillside writes directions for Greta on a fish skin.

Back in the cabin I smell the paper again, and this time it smells like dry fish in a cold underground house. Of course, it could be just the general smell in the air from all the fish I've boiled here. I grab a stack of moldy paper and a pencil from a shelf. I know what this story says already. This time I'm going to write my own.

❋

"For whom do you wander?" asks the bent old crone. "For whom do you search?"

And then Greta, who's taken leave of her senses in the warmth of the buried home, remembers her sweet friend and the ice that had lodged in his heart. It is time to be gone, to be searching once again. She knows that's what she came for, though she no longer understands why. Maybe, since her friend left, she should accept his decision and believe that's what it is. After all, she has no proof otherwise.

But in the end, she begs forgiveness from the old woman for being unable to tarry. That very morning, before the moon sinks below the horizon, Greta will journey, she's decided, to the Castle of the Snow Queen, far away toward the gray line of horizon.

As she shuts the old woman's door, the wind grabs it and rips the handle from her hands. Smoke from the chimney blows flat, in a sheet, along the ground. Snowflakes, however, are not falling but jump about like popcorn on a hot stove. Greta laughs and catches several with her tongue before moving away from the safety of the now invisible shelter onto the white trackless plain.

But as Greta ventures out from the mound containing the old woman's home, she finds caribou tracks, a sign that other creatures have wandered this way. At first she sees only a few, then troughs through the snow where great wild herds have trotted. Greta can stay on these trails by the feel of hard-packed snow under her feet. And as she wends her way down the invisible route, her thoughts fly to her friend and his frozen heart and the wickedness of the

Queen who led him so far astray. As the night passes, creatures of the taiga stare out from the storm so Greta sees only the shining of their eyes for a moment through the swirling flakes of snow; then darkness breaks about them.

Greta is cold but she is also content. There's nowhere on this Earth she'd rather be. Something in her heart answers the wildness of the storm. How unfortunate, she thinks, that I am seeking a friend who perhaps doesn't even care to be sought. How lacking in good fortune that this fierce beauty cannot penetrate my own heart, that the fate of the old crone in need of a helper cannot move me as does the fate of my long-departed friend.

Because that's the question, I think: at what point should you just give up?

That night I dream I'm in a blizzard. On the horizon is a yellow light. Sky and earth are invisible. Without my boots planted in the snow, I couldn't tell earth and sky apart. The air in between is crowded with falling snowflakes. I brush them from my shoulders, take off my hat and bang it against my legs. Dad is on the trail beside me, laughing as always. "Cold enough for you?" he says.

I wake knowing I have to look for tracks around the cabin, check if the bear has come back. I've never heard of a bear stalking a person this way. I've had enough, I think, enough of being scared.

All this time I've been frightened not so much of the bear, but of the panic, the horrible surge of terror I felt when he was near. Panic is instant; it can't be controlled. But the bear's not a monster; he's a living creature. I can look at him and see him as just a bear.

If I look at him long enough and hard enough, I might still be afraid. But maybe he'll feel like what he really is, a fellow sojourner on this Earth with a perspective all his own.

Before leaving the cabin, I fry up a huge breakfast of rice and jerky that I've marinated for days in water, brown sugar and spices. I'm starving all the time these days.

Really, I don't want to shoot him, even after he hurt Brooks. I want that golden bear to dig out his den and hunker down to sleep while the snow drifts around his bed. I want him to grow thin and his heartbeat to slow. Of course, he has to fatten first, though not on me and not on my dog.

I'm going caribou hunting downriver again tomorrow. And the bear will simply have to stay out of my way.

18

In the End

That day we climb the mountain directly behind the cabin. I scramble, holding on to aspen trunks when it's steep, up the slope to the ridge and then along it. A white powder from the aspens lingers on my hands, feeling soft like baby powder when I rub it in. Brooks barely limps. As always in high country, the world below is miniaturized. Though I scan thoroughly below us, I see nothing except an eagle and a flock of redpolls still in the trees. Whistling, I start back down, stones scuffling underfoot.

Directly below me, where Brooks is sniffing, a head shakes. I draw my father's rifle and shoot over the head.

The bear was sleeping, hidden under an overhang. Before the echo of the rifle dies, he's charging.

He stops before us. This time Brooks shakes behind my legs. I feel them vibrate.

I chamber another shell. My hands are shaking too. Nah, my whole body is trembling from the inside out.

"Whoa, bear."

How can it be the same bear that Brooks harassed on the mountain, that I've glimpsed again and again?

But it is. I've never even heard of another with yellow striping its back.

Figure out why the bear's charging, Becky told me, and that will tell you what to do. Is it an offensive or a defensive attack?

Words have fled from me; they're streaming off like the wind from the peaks. There's just panic now and the eyes of the bear and its hot breath and the snow crunching under his paws. He's walking toward us slowly with head swaying. My eyes go from his mouth to his claws and back again. This time I'd run if I could. Like in a nightmare, my feet won't work.

"Whoa, bear." I say it loudly and clearly. Speak firmly but without yelling.

Brooks growls.

"Stay," I order.

The bear steps steadily forward, legs slightly bowed out.

I peer down the barrel and line up the notch and bead. I inhale deeply and hold it in for steadiness. I can only shoot over his head once more. Then it has to be for real. The shot explodes into the autumn air.

But the bear doesn't run.

"Scat," I shout. My voice is as loud as the rifle it seems. Mom, I think. Please come. Now. Be here behind me.

Black lips draw back. The bear stands on back legs and snuffles his snout in our direction. Such an unusual hide would be worth a fortune. No one could blame me for shooting. It's a level playing field here: The bear's been stalking us. He's injured my dog. He's kept me awake at night.

Now suddenly it's clear.

The forest about me is absolutely still.

I shoot.

I shoot at the ground before the bear's massive paws. A scuff of snow flies up. In the next moment I lean the rifle against a tree trunk and grab my bear spray from my coat pocket where I've kept it warm. I pull off the safety clip, and this time I walk toward the bear.

Not away. I'm through with walking away.

"Stay, Brooks."

Brooks stays.

The bear is still standing on his hind legs, watching me. I hear his teeth clacking.

"Enough, bear," I tell him, low and deep. Another step. I've never felt so strong, so at peace. Why was I scared? Who has the best defenses here? It isn't the bear carrying the gun or the gunpowder bangers or the pepper spray. He has teeth and claws and a fierce need to eat before he dens.

And I have a fierce need too: a need to live my life.

I step steadily forward, holding the red can of spray at arm's length. And I have Brooks, wounded already. This time I'll protect him.

I depress the nozzle, and capsicum pepper streams into the bear's eyes and up his nostrils.

He snorts and tosses his head, dropping to the ground.

I ease up, not breathing. In this moment, I'm alive. Maybe I won't be tomorrow, but I don't care anymore. It's a fine autumn day, sparkling with sun and fresh snow. Today while the Earth is turning, I get to be alive on it. And I'm glad.

The bear tears at his eyes with a front paw. His claws are knives ready to slice off my skin.

I spray again.

Whimpering like a dog, he lumbers off into the trees. I jump backward to the rifle, chamber a shell and with one motion, I shoot. I aim into the ground behind his fleeing rump, golden stripe metallic in the sunshine.

"It's your own bloody fault if it hurts, bear. You could have let us be."

He'll get over it. He'll be just fine.

And so will we.

Brooks presses nervously against my leg the entire walk back to the cabin. I can't stop laughing out loud.

"The bear went over the mountain," I sing...Dad went over the mountain too. I knew all along, I think, that I couldn't find him or ever really know why he disappeared. All I needed was to know that he wanted to come home.

There's not going to be any closure here, so I might as well just believe that he loved me, that he didn't mean to leave me. So many fathers in this world would die for their children; mine didn't even bother to stick around.

I can't put any of it together. I can't juggle those particular balls.

The blue sky today is enormous. We've got jerky and plenty of dry food, and tomorrow I'll try caribou hunting again. Mom will be here—for the life of me I can't remember how many days more until she comes.

I've written my own version of "The Snow Queen." I know what happened to Greta, struggling valiantly across the tundra toward her old friend. She started to love the journey: the ice and snow and the troughs of caribou tracks and the endless stars and lights above.

I don't know what the ending will be yet, but it will come. And when I finish writing, I'll move on to the next story. And the next.

"And what do you think he saw?" I sing. "He saw another mountain, he saw another mountain, he saw another mountain and what do you think he did?"

Brooks bays along, almost collapsed against me.

"The bear went over the mountain," I repeat. I stop. "Guess what, Brooks. I think he actually did."

It's a long carefree life ahead without a bear lying in wait. Mountains beyond mountains are waiting to be explored.

Suddenly I can hardly wait.

Back at the cabin I shake the cardboard quote from its book, meaning to tack it back on the wall.

A small black notebook, lodged behind the bookshelf all these years, thuds to the floor.

I recognize it at once. It's the diary I gave Dad before he left.

For a long minute I don't move. Can I live with what he has to say? Can I be happy? Live a good life?

And when I do pick it up, I turn at once to the last entry.

Rained all day again. I heard my name on the radio tonight and tried to answer, but something's wrong. It won't transmit. I'm starting home tomorrow so they won't worry. I think it's time anyway. I feel so much better. And I miss them. I never knew how much I loved them until I left.

So now I know. He never meant to stay away at all. He tried to keep his word.

I climb into bed, whistle for Brooks, who can jump up himself now, and blow out the lamp. I'll read the rest later with Mom and Becky—it's their story too.

"Good night, Dad," I whisper. "Sweet dreams."

Epilogue

That night—my last alone, it turns out—I juggle fire on the gravel bar under the northern lights. Vast curtains of red and green aurora sweep across the starry sky.

This time I know how to keep the sticks alight. I cut sections of one of Dad's old leather belts and wrap each piece around the end of one of the three spruce torches I've whittled. I douse the ends with kerosene from a five-gallon bucket left in the shed. Then I light a bonfire and hold my homemade torches in the blaze. The shooting flames make me jump but I don't let go. A skiff of snow dusts the stones around my fire-pit when I begin but soon melts.

This is what it must be like to be in charge of the universe: juggling all those people who are blazing their courses through the air, juggling planets, galaxies and suns.

So what if one burns out? So what if a child's father doesn't make it; if, in the course of blazing across his own sky, he just fizzles out and lands somewhere nobody ever finds him?

Does anyone even notice?

My torches are true to the center and falling down the sides, like water, like the northern lights, like sand dunes and rock slides, over and over. The same forces act on all flesh, on all pieces of the Earth.

And now I've had enough of fire breathing in my face.

I let the torches drop, one at a time, and there under the dancing aurora I rest my fire sticks in the bonfire coals and reach for my juggling balls instead.

It's bright as day with the lights and the stars and a full moon floating above the river's ice. The northern lights come from particles streaming through the atmosphere from the sun. Dad told me that.

I slip the balls under my legs, under each other, slipping and sliding in patterns so fast that even if someone were watching they couldn't follow. My brain can't even track the patterns. If I stopped to think, the balls would crash onto stone.

And now I remember the story I made up before I left Mom and Becky at home. I remember a princess who couldn't leave her castle, how she circled and turned, again and again. How she found her own magic place outside the castle grounds, but it wasn't far enough away. Nightingales sang in it. A stream trickled through green, green moss.

"Go, princess," I shout, and the balls dance by the flames of my fire. Oh, it's not so easy leaving the castle. It's not so easy being free. If I were in charge of this universe, what would I do differently?

And then one ball falls and then another. I don't even pick them up. Up the bank and back in the forest along the trail, the cabin is glowing with lamplight: *The princess picked her way through the wall of trees and it grew even darker, but still she traveled on, and in the end a hut appeared, glowing softly in the darkness.*

It was her home.

I've changed my own ending.

I could say it's the last fairy-tale ending I'll ever change, but I know it isn't. My life won't be long enough to rewrite them all, whichever way I choose. And that's the magic key that unlocks the gate into the forest. Whichever way I choose.

Yes, my father is dead. He no longer lives in the forest by a river somewhere. But he tried to come home. He loved me fiercely. That's the secret I needed to know.

I miss him. And every morning and every evening I'll stop whatever I am doing so I can really focus on missing him. I won't pretend that I don't, even if it's embarrassing to still care.

I'll stare at the stars at night and I'll chant while the balls cascade up the middle and down the outside. Until one day maybe I'll get tired of it. Enough, I'll say, and I'll ride away to find my destiny, snatching his baseball cap to wear as I ride. Even then, when I hear a whisper of missing him, I'll pull on the reins and stay very still and listen to it.

That's the only way to mourn someone, to mourn them until the grief flies away. Then hold your hands to catch it when it returns. Don't flinch even when the flames hover above your face.

My father never meant to stay away. He wanted to return. Northern lights cascade across the dark dome of sky like a moving river of light.

Brooks, on the far side of the bonfire, wakes, shakes and wanders over, poking his nose against my leg so I'll pat him. He makes a sound in his throat like a siren warming up, and I remember leaving the highway with him so long ago. We did it, Brooks and I.

We came home.

And that's as far as the fairy tale ever gets.

Acknowledgments

With thanks to my large and rather noisy family, whose presence in this world is my home, especially to Mikin, Elizabeth and Mary, whom I delight in every day. And finally my gratitude to the Dempster Mountains for the stories they tell me when the wind blows.

Born in Great Britain, Joanne Bell grew up in New Brunswick, Alberta and British Columbia. She visited Dawson City, Yukon, many years ago and fell in love with the nearby Ogilvie Mountains, where she spent years running dogs, hiking, canoeing and living in log cabins. Now married with two daughters, she works as a naturalist in the summers and is a substitute teacher in Dawson City whenever she is not in the mountains. She spends as much time as possible in her log cabin about twenty miles from the Dempster Highway.